FRIGHT
INTO
FLIGHT

Also by Amber Fallon:

The Terminal
The Warblers
TV Dinners from Hell

FRIGHT INTO FLIGHT

EDITED BY AMBER FALLON

WORD HORDE
PETALUMA, CA

First Edition

ISBN: 978-1-939905-44-4

A Word Horde Book
www.wordhorde.com

TABLE OF CONTENTS

For women everywhere, may you spread your wings and soar.

NOW BOARDING: YOUR TICKET TO TERROR

AMBER FALLON

irports, like doctors' offices, inspire dread, anxiety, and fear just by the very fact of their existence. Sure, they're responsible for an awful lot of good things. Things like vacations, family reunions, new job opportunities, honeymoons, and holidays. But that's not what we think of, is it? Not when that little *Fasten Seatbelts!* sign lights up and the plane starts to move just before takeoff, and certainly not midflight, when turbulence jolts the aircraft and we're all forced to remember that we're stuck inside a little metal tube that somehow decided to defy gravity to keep us aloft.

Even before the nightmare tragedy of 9/11 taught us that airplanes could be used as weapons to terrifying effect, and potentially panic-inducing things like TSA screenings were put into place, people have been afraid to leave the ground.

A quick search of the web reveals fear of flying to be in the top ten most common phobias again and again and again. Obviously, that leads one to conclude that a lot of people have a lot of fear regarding air travel, even though it's statistically safer than driving a car.

i

Maybe there's a reason for that.

Maybe, somewhere deep down in our reptilian brains, we know that the sky doesn't belong to us humans. We might borrow it sometimes, poke our shiny skyscrapers and our pretty parachutes into its blue vastness, but we will never truly own it.

Not like *they* do: the terrors that have made it their home. The beasts that fly and shriek and rend their prey into bite-sized pieces while somehow remaining in midair as if it were nothing. The things that inspire that quakey-quavery panic jelly feeling in our knees even as our brains urge us to *run!*

But maybe I'm getting ahead of myself. Perhaps, just perhaps, some of us do hold a claim on the sky above.

Women have long been associated with flight. Angels are often (but not always!) depicted as female, as are fairies. And of course, we have the brave Valkyries and the bloodthirsty harpies to count among our number. Surely, there are pilots, astronauts, stewardesses, barnstormers, and skydivers among us as well. Legions of women throughout history have screamed our names into that vast beyond, so loudly that some still echo.

Within the pages of this book, you'll find a variety of stories that are as unique and beautiful as clouds in a summer sky, but just like clouds can portend dark skies and stormy weather sometimes within the blink of an eye, these stories have a dark side.

Gathered here for your enjoyment is a collection of tales unified by the overall theme of flight. Within the boundless expanse of that theme, these women have spread their wings and soared, creating some truly wonderful and (terrifying!) tales, stories of angels and demons, witches and warriors, monsters and heroes, sure to make anyone glance warily up at the sky after reading them.

So make sure you have your ticket ready and your government-issued ID out. You won't want to miss this!

Amber Fallon
Boston, Massachusetts April 2018

THE FLOATING GIRLS: A DOCUMENTARY

DAMIEN ANGELICA WALTERS

The floating girls are all but forgotten now. It's easier to pretend they didn't exist, to pretend it didn't happen. But there are parents who still keep bedrooms captured in time, complete with clothes folded in bureau drawers and diaries tucked beneath pillows, everything in its place, waiting, and there are friends who still gaze at the sky, wondering how far the girls floated and if they ever fell.

Some of us haven't forgotten. Some of us never will.

***

Twelve years ago, three hours after the sun set on the second of August, nearly 300,000 girls between the ages of eleven and seventeen vanished. Eyewitness reports state that the girls floated away, yet even now, many of those eyewitnesses have recanted their stories or simply refuse to talk about it at all.

The girls lived in cities, in the suburbs, in the country. They lived in first world and third world countries. They were only children; they were one of many siblings; they were of all ethnicities and religious backgrounds. They were everyone and anyone, and after that night in August, they were no more.

I've found plenty of evidence decrying the phenomenon, but there are lists of the girls who disappeared. Those who claim it's all bullshit provide other lists, girls who vanished and were found years later: the runaways; the girls involved in ugly custody battles, who were spirited away by either custodial or non-custodial parents; the girls whose decomposing bodies were recovered from forests, old drainpipes, beneath concrete patios.

But none of those girls were floating girls, only gone girls. The reports always conveniently leave that out.

I wonder about the evidence I haven't found, that doesn't exist. It seems like there should be so much more. And how many girls who vanished were never reported? And why just girls? Why just these girls?

As far as I can tell, very few scientists or statisticians studied the phenomenon itself. No one counseled the families; no one dug through the chaos to find the facts. Like certain religious or political scandals, everyone wanted to brush it under the rug.

Maybe it made a strange sort of sense at the time. I don't know.

***

Jessie and I grew up next door in a tiny corner of suburbia. You know the sort: backyard cookouts, running through the sprinklers, drinking water from the hose, playing tag. Perfectly charming. The sort of childhood that screams ideal. The sort of childhood that could take place anywhere, in any town, not just our little corner in Baltimore, Maryland.

Our back yards were separated by a row of hedges with spaces in between perfectly sized for someone to walk through. We would flit from yard to yard—mine had the swing set and the sprinkler; hers the sandbox and hammock—and house to house—split foyer for me, rancher for her—nearly inseparable, spinning circles and holding hands while we chanted Jessie and Tracy, best friends forever.

My strongest memories are of the countless hours we spent catching fireflies. We'd keep them inside glass jars with holes poked in the lids so they wouldn't die and invent stories that they were princesses trapped in the bodies and the lights were their way of calling for help because they couldn't speak. And every night before we had to go in, we'd let them go, watching until they blinked out of sight, pretending they were off to find their mothers, their princes, the witches who'd cursed them.

I think you only truly make that kind of friendship in childhood. When you get older, you know better than to let people in. You know they'll only disappoint you in the end.

***

Video interview with Karen Michaels of Monmouth, Oregon, March 17, 2010:

[A woman sits in a cramped, dingy kitchen, a lit cigarette clutched tightly between two fingers, an overflowing ashtray by her side. She grimaces at the camera and looks away. Her face is worn and heavily lined, her shoulders hunched forward.]

"Thank you for agreeing to talk to me, Mrs. Michaels. I know this is difficult."

[Mrs. Michaels takes a drag from her cigarette. Exhales the smoke loudly.]

"Call me Karen, okay?"

"Okay, Karen. I know it's been a long time, but can you tell me what happened that night, August second—"

[She waves the hand holding the cigarette.]

"I know what night you're talking about."

[Another inhale from her cigarette. Another exhale.]

"Nina had problems with sleepwalking when she was a kid. Used to drive me crazy. For a couple years, I had to lock her bedroom door from the outside to keep her in the house. You got kids?"

"No—"

"That's right. You already told me you didn't. Who knows, maybe you're lucky. Anyway, that night, the night Nina floated, it had been years since she walked in her sleep. I heard her go down the steps, and I followed her. She went out the front door and stood on the lawn, staring down at her feet, like this."

[Mrs. Michaels stubs out her cigarette and stands with her arms straight and her head down, her hands held out a few inches from her body.]

"I thought she was sleepwalking again, that's all, so I stayed on the front porch. I was getting ready to go get her, grab her arm, and take her back in because I had to get up early in the morning. But then she went up, just up, like a balloon. I, I—"

[Video cuts off. Returns. Mrs. Michaels is wiping her eyes.]

"Are you sure you're okay?"

"Yeah, sure, I'm fine. I, so she went up, and I thought…I don't know what I thought. I ran and tried to grab her, but she was already up too far. I touched the side of her foot, but I guess, I guess I was just too late."

[She grabs another cigarette and lights it. Her voice is barely audible when she speaks again.]

"I let her go. I didn't know what else to do, so I let her go."

[Her head snaps up. She looks straight into the camera.]

"Everyone told me not to talk about it. It's like she never existed at all. But she did, and no one cared that she was gone. No one. Do you really think this thing, your project, will help?"

"I'd like to think it will, yes."

[She makes a sound low in her throat.]

"Will you tell me what Nina was like?"

"She was like every other kid. Listened to her music too loud, left her dirty clothes on the floor, griped about her chores, but she didn't run around wild or anything like that. She didn't drink or do drugs or cause me any grief."

"And what was your relationship with Nina like?"

"Normal. I mean, we had fights, but nothing really serious. She was always in her room, reading or listening to music."

"What about with her siblings, her father?"

"Everyone was fine. Everything was fine."

[There's a long pause, and she looks away with tears in her eyes. Video ends.]

***

Jessie's father died the year we turned eight. I remember black clothing, tears, confusion, and the smell of flowers. At some point, she and I snuck out into her back yard and played in the sandbox. I don't remember what we talked about or if we talked about anything at all, but I remember how we slipped out of our dress shoes and wriggled our toes through the warm top layer of sand to the cool beneath. I remember the scent of honeysuckle thick in the air.

***

Recording of a telephone interview, July 28, 2012:

"You're not going to use my name, right? I don't want you to use my name."

"No, I won't."

"Good. Okay."

"Tell me what you think happened on the night of August second."

"All I can tell you is what I saw. The kid was hanging in the air in her yard, looking like some kind of angel, only not the kind you can see through. I mean, she wasn't wearing anything like an angel would. I think she had on some kind of dress, but nothing like you see in pictures of angels or anything like that. Then she went straight up. Craziest damn thing I ever saw. I kept thinking it was the beer. I only had a couple, maybe three, but …"

"Did you do anything?"

"What could I do? Hell, by the time I figured out my eyes wasn't playing tricks, she was high up. I mean really high."

"And you told the authorities what you saw?"

"Yeah, I told them. Lot of good that did. They said I was crazy. Or drunk. People can't float. But I know what I saw, and that girl just floated up and away."

"Did you know anything about her?"

"No, she was just the kid who lived next door. She kept to herself, the whole family did. I mean they were nice enough, just not real friendly."

"Is there anything else you'd like to say?"

"You're not going to use my name for this thing, right? I don't want my name used."

"No, sir. As I said before, I won't use your name."

***

Jessie and I started to drift apart the summer she turned eleven, about a year after her mom remarried. I'd ask her to come over and catch fireflies, and she'd say no. I'd invite her to spend the night, and she'd say no. I spent countless nights crying, trying to figure out what I'd done wrong, because best friends didn't stop talking to each other unless something was wrong.

My mother sat me down and said, "Tracy, honey, that's what happens with friends sometimes. Don't worry. Maybe she's just going through a phase. You are becoming young women, you know."

She was only trying to help, but I wanted everything to go back to the way it had been, not the way it was.

***

Video footage, dated August 2, 2002:

Video opens with a scene of a back yard, complete with a hot tub, a fire pit, and tables and chairs set up for a party. There's a break in the video; when it returns, the sky is dark and a party is in full swing. No children are present. The camera captures several people saying hello to the cameraman, there's another break in the filming, and then the camera is stationary, capturing a wide view of the partygoers.

5 minutes, 06 seconds: A pale blotch can be seen in the far left corner, above a row of well-trimmed hedges.

5 minutes, 08 seconds: The pale blotch is larger, the shape completely visible over the hedge.

5 minutes, 10 seconds: While the partygoers continue to drink and laugh, the blotch continues to rise.

Video editing enhancement of the last few seconds before the blotch disappears from the film clearly shows a young girl in her early teens, her face solemn, rising up through the air.

[Note: Records state the video was taken by Jack Stevenson of Denver, Colorado. Repeated attempts to contact Mr. Stevenson have been unsuccessful.]

***

By the time I was twelve, the drift between Jessie and I had become a crevasse. We weren't even on speaking terms. She was just a girl I used to know. As kids do, I'd made new friends and sure, her rejection hurt and sometimes I'd look over the fence to see if she was outside, but I was a kid, just a stupid kid.

How was I supposed to know?

***

Photograph A: Photo shows a baobab tree and a girl beside it. On closer inspection, the girl's feet are hovering about a foot from the ground. The girl is looking away from the camera. The back of the photograph reads August 2, Shurugwi, Zimbabwe.

[Note: Photograph provided by one of the girl's family members, who asked to remain anonymous. For that reason, the name of the girl is also withheld.]

Photograph B: The central image is the Eiffel Tower in Paris, France. On the far right of the photo, a girl is suspended in the air, her arms held in the distinct way described by many others, her face serene. Using the tower as a point of measure, she is approximately 1,050 feet in the air.

[Note: Image found on a website claiming it was manipulated digitally, however, no evidence of alteration can be found in the image itself. The girl in the photograph has not yet been identified.]

Photograph C: Photo of Trakai Castle, south of Vilnius, Lithuania, taken by Algimantas Serunis of Chicago, Illinois, while on vacation. A girl's head and shoulders are visible above the westernmost tower of the castle.

[Note: The girl has been tentatively identified as Ruta Gremaila. Attempts to contact her family have been unsuccessful.]

***

When I was fourteen, Jessie showed up at the back door one night. I was blaring music and eating the last of the mint chocolate chip ice cream, knowing my dad would pretend to make a big deal about the empty container and my mom would roll her eyes at both of us. My parents weren't home, and yes, I've wondered more than once if it would've made a difference.

"Yeah?" I remember saying.

"I was wondering if maybe you'd want to hang out for a little bit?" she asked, her voice whisper-thin, her eyes all red and puffy, like she'd been crying. Behind the red, though, there was a strange emptiness, a hollow where laughter had once lived.

I remember being surprised, more at her request than her eyes. Although I'd made new friends, she hadn't. She skulked through the halls at school like a ghost. She sat alone in the cafeteria at lunchtime and with her shoulders hunched in class. She wore baggy clothing and kept her head down so her hair almost covered her face, and she always walked home alone.

"I can't, sorry. I have a math test tomorrow I have to study for."

"Oh, okay." She stood for a minute, toeing the doormat with the tip of her shoe. "See you around then?"

"Sure."

But I lied. There was no math test. I just didn't want to talk to her.

***

Video footage of interview with Sheriff Joseph Miller, Brookhaven, Pennsylvania, September 9, 2008:

"No, none of it's true. I have no idea why you'd even want to talk about it."

"So why do you think everyone reported the same thing?"

"I don't have an answer to that."

"Maybe it's because it really happened."

[He glares into the camera.]

"Look, it didn't happen. A bunch of kids ran away, a bunch more people got upset and invented some story about floating."

"But didn't three girls from your own town vanish?"

[His expression changes, and he crosses his arms over his chest.]

"Yeah."

"Don't you think that's suspect?"

"Sometimes kids, especially girls, run away together. It happens."

"And what if I told you those girls weren't even friends, didn't even go to the same schools?"

[He sighs heavily, looks at some spot in the distance, and shakes his head in dismissal.]

"We're done here. Some of us have real work to do."

***

On August 2, 2002, the summer Jessie and I were fifteen, I was out back on a blanket, staring at the stars, waiting for one to fall so I could make a wish. My parents were out at the movies, and other than the crickets chirping, the neighborhood was quiet.

Jessie's kitchen door opened—it had a funny little squeak that all the oil in the world wouldn't fix—and Jessie walked out into the yard. The lights in her house were off, and she was little more than a shadow flitting across the grass.

I hunched down on the blanket and watched through the

hedges. She stood still in the middle of her yard for several minutes with her head down, her hands fisted at her sides. I thought about calling her name—I know I did—but then her hands relaxed, her arms extended slightly, and she lifted her chin to stare straight ahead. Then she lifted off the ground.

She was a foot in the air before I realized it wasn't an illusion, before I was able to do anything other than blink. I scrambled to my feet, told her to stop, and raced through the hedges, scratching my upper arms all to hell in the process. I shouted her name and called out for my parents, for her parents, for anyone.

Jessie never looked down, not once. I stood right underneath her, waving my arms and yelling at her to come back, until my legs couldn't hold me up anymore and my throat was too thick to speak.

My parents found me in the yard when they got home. I was on the blanket, sitting with my grass-stained knees pulled to my chin, crying. I told them how Jessie just floated and kept floating until I couldn't see her anymore, until she was gone.

I saw the disbelief in their eyes. My father went over to Jessie's house, knocked on the door, and came back shrugging his shoulders after no one answered. My mom pressed her hand against my forehead, proclaimed I had a fever, and sent me to bed. I stayed there for three days.

Jessie's parents told the police she ran away.

***

Video footage of an attempted interview on August 18, 2011 with John Gelvin from Brawley, California, whose daughter, Rosie, age thirteen, is still listed as missing. Documents show she was reported as a floating girl. Other documents show that Child Protective Services had been called on at least one occasion before Rosie's disappearance, but no further action from CPS can be found.

"Sir, you said you saw Rosie float."

"No. I didn't. You're mistaken. She ran away."

"But I have a report here, a police report, that says—"

[He spins around and begins to walk away, speaking over his shoulder.]

"Leave me alone. Just leave me alone."

***

I tried to tell people the truth. My parents continued to blame the fever. When I told Jessie's parents, her mother's eyes filled with tears, the silent, terrifying kind; her stepfather told me to leave their house and never come back. They moved away a few months later and didn't tell anyone where they were going.

People at school thought I was crazy, even after the other reports came out. Jessie was just another troubled kid who ran away. It happened every day. No big deal.

If I'd been an adult, if I hadn't see Jessie float away, I wonder if I would've been as dismissive. Possibly. Probably.

I tried to tell the truth so many times, but no one would listen.

***

Graffiti on the side of a building in Rapid City, South Dakota, June 8, 2013, in the section of the city known as Art Alley:

SILENCE IS A FORM OF HELIUM

[Note: According to a local artist, who asked not to be named, the graffiti was originally written on the building in September of 2002, and she's been repainting it as needed ever since. When asked if she knew the identity of the original artist or thought that the statement was related to the floating girls, she declined to answer.]

***

Eventually I stopped talking about it, about Jessie. I didn't forget her, but it was too hard to keep trying to explain what I saw to people who refused to believe it. I finished high school, moved out of state for college, dropped out in my second year, and came back home.

When my parents decided to sell their house and move to Florida, I found a box of photos in the attic, pictures of me and Jessie when we were young, pictures of us holding our firefly jars, grinning crazy kid smiles, those smiles that scream innocence. Our eyes were filled with laughter and happiness and hope.

And I remembered her eyes the night she came over, the night I turned her away. We all have a secret spot, a tiny light, inside us, and it doesn't take much to make that light go out. It doesn't take much to extinguish that light forever.

As I carried the photos out to my car, I decided to do something. I'm not sure if I decided to do it for Jessie or for the others or for me, but I don't think it matters.

I'm not a fifteen-year-old girl anymore, and I've spent years digging for proof, searching for the truth. Maybe now people will listen, and maybe they'll start talking.

***

Excerpt from "A Study into the Phenomenon of the Floating Girls," dated November 2002, author not cited:

Given a lack of concrete evidence to the phenomenon, and with evidence that a percentage of the girls were from troubled homes and had a history of running away, we can only conclude there was no phenomenon, only a strange set of coincidental circumstances.

It is also noted that there was a heavy incident of fog in the northwestern states, which may explain the visual oddities noted there.

Reports from other countries are sketchy at best with most being reported well after the disappearances in the United States, leading this researcher to determine that they were copying the phenomenon, perhaps in hope of cashing in on the notoriety. More research is needed.

[Note: There is no evidence that any further research was conducted.]

***

I live twenty minutes away from the house I grew up in. Kids still play in sandboxes, they still catch fireflies and run through sprinklers, they still promise to be best friends forever. At night, I stare at the sky and wonder if the girls are still floating. I think they are, and we just can't see them.

I tell Jessie I'm sorry, but the words seem so fucking inadequate. I should've been there for her. I should've listened. And after, I should've kept talking. Hell, I should've screamed and shouted. But I didn't.

No one did.

For Jessie
Tracy Richardson, Director
The Floating Girls Project
Baltimore, Maryland
2014

I DID IT FOR THE ART

IZZY LEE

Kira snapped her gum and groaned as the Hummer H2 barreled down Connecticut Route 45, the vehicle spitting twigs and pebbles beneath its enormous wheels.

"Something the matter?" Jeff asked, eyeing her in the rearview mirror.

The platinum blond Ukrainian thirteen-year-old model mumbled: "Bored."

She slouched in the back seat, her freakishly long legs stretched up over the console beside him. Spanish twelve-year-old Mariana lay slumped against the opposite window, half her face concealed beneath a floppy black '70s Boho hat and large Jackie O. sunglasses. Earbuds trailed from her long dark hair—the only giveaway that she lived in the twenty-first century. She wore heeled mahogany suede boots and a blood-red peasant dress decorated with embroidered flowers.

These girls get older every day.

His eyes lingered on Mariana's exposed cream-white shoulder, a seductive contrast to the color of her dress. He felt someone watching him and glanced over at Lesley, the Upper East Side fourteen-year-old brunette in the passenger seat. She'd

15

caught him gaping. Those damn heirs and their own personal Camelots; they'd learned to play every game under the Madison Avenue sun from their socialite mothers and uppity private girl school cliques. He'd make sure she wasn't so dignified by the time she returned home.

Jeff cleared his throat and focused on the road. This seemed to satisfy Lesley's propriety and she went back to typing on her phone. He imagined her taking requests in a schoolgirl outfit behind the bleachers—super-short plaid skirt, knee-high socks, and crisp white shirt tied at the waist. More so, he imagined it was him ramming her into oblivion.

Down, boy. They were too close to the location, and he'd have to stand up soon. He conjured up images of his parents wasting away at the old folks' home to dampen his desire. Just the way they smelled, that weird elderly rot, was enough to make him soft.

They passed a sign for Mohawk Mountain, just a few miles ahead.

"We're almost there, girls," he grinned.

"Good," Kira sniffed. "I have to pee."

Jeff suppressed a smirk and a golden shower fantasy as the Hummer shot onto Interstate 7, through Cornwall Bridge and then down Bald Mountain Road—formerly Dark Entry Road— before careening onto a smaller country route.

***

The faded white Housatonic Bed & Breakfast sign swung slightly from its hinges above them as he pulled into the driveway and turned the ignition off. "Now remember—" he turned and looked each of the girls in the eye. "You say nothing of the hair and make-up we just got done in the city. But especially this—if they ask, we're NOT going to Dudleytown. You're my daughter,

Lesley, who brought your friends along. We're just up here for a fun hike and maybe to take some photos."

The models all mumbled in agreement as they got out of the Hummer with their overnight bags, which really held designer skivvies for the shoot. Jeff thought again about what he'd like to do to his "daughter for the day," and what the innkeepers might think about that. He imagined taking her right there on the porch while they looked on. It'd be a hell of an advertisement for the desolate establishment in the middle of nowhere.

Maybe he could convince Kira into some fun later. She seemed like she might be into it—the younger models usually were, especially if they were foreign. They didn't know any better, and they thought that he could help them with their careers. Working with him usually did, even though he had a reputation for sleaziness. High-profile designers and magazine editors in the fashion industry knew of his fondness for young girls, but they just didn't care, especially because they liked his work and that he was well known. They had their own secrets, too. In fact, several of the top designers and editors spent their spare time stowed away with young boys just as much as he did with the girls. Jeff's work was good and it sold clothes—metric tons of hideously overpriced goods to the world's elite. Besides, if Kira wasn't game, the roofies and ecstasy tabs were practically burning a hole in his pocket.

***

After they checked in, they headed upstairs to their suite. It was country chinz all the way—a vomitorium of white doily grandma chic and indigo floral print. No respecting New Yorker would be caught dead here, but they weren't staying anyway.

"All right, freshen up if you need to, but wear the first set of lingerie underneath your clothes. The rest you'll change into on location, but be quick about it—we've gotta catch the light while it lasts." Jeff sat down on the loveseat and pretended to fiddle with his lenses while he watched Mariana and Kira change beneath his mirrored aviators. Lesley had gone into the bathroom and locked the door, the prude. Maybe he'd slip her one of the roofies first. Would she be watching her water bottle?

Wait—the wine! Jeff smirked and pulled plastic cups and a bottle from one of his gear bags. Alcohol was always good for loosening girls up before a shoot. If he was lucky, he'd be deflowering virgins today.

Kira wiggled out of her tunic and leggings—she wore nothing beneath, a good sign that she wasn't scared of sex like a lot of girls—or Americans, for that matter. Mariana followed suit, and they both slipped on the filmy chiffon bra and panty sets, and then their regular outfits.

While they were busy, he poured the cabernet. Hmm... If he roofied them too early, they wouldn't be able to pose well. He settled on just the wine, and when Lesley came out of the bathroom, he gave full cups to all three girls. Although they were young city models—already used to being objectified—he was amazed at what he could get away with, due to his talent. What dumb parents they had. If anyone ever really questioned his motives, he could say that he did it for the art, and he wouldn't be lying, not completely.

"To art," he said, and raised his glass.

***

They trudged though the backyard and beyond into the woods. Jeff's backpack and camera bag hung heavy from his shoulders, bulging with camera equipment, industrial chain link cutters, and another bottle of red. After a short walk, an old fence adorned with a rusted red DO NOT TRESPASS sign appeared. Not one to comply with vacant authority symbols, Jeff made short work of the tangled steel. It wasn't easy cutting through the metal; he got a bit sweaty, but that was okay. The physical display showed off his masculinity. He already knew that his tight jeans hugged his lower body well—a flirty male make-up artist had told him so, hoping to get him to switch teams. Ha. He had let the guy suck him off, however. A warm mouth was a warm mouth.

After he'd cut a good-sized opening, he held part of the chain-link fence back to let the girls through and mentally patted himself on the back for his chivalry. Not one of them thanked him, much to his chagrin. Maybe they'd be more grateful after the gallery opening and glossy fashion spread for one of the world's leading magazines, and after they got a billion bookings. But he'd be getting something in return. That's how this industry worked.

***

An overgrown clearing rose up ahead. It was obvious that there had been a settlement of sorts here once; several crumbled foundations dotted the landscape, enough to fill a small colonial town. He looked up at the cloud cover that presented a lovely, natural diffused light, and grinned. "Perfect. All right— let's get to it."

He uncapped his lens, adjusted the aperture, and focused. The girls stripped down to the designer lingerie and like coy automatons, began to pose. This was going to be good. They were young, but they learned fast—the long, svelte bodies twisted and paused—sometimes perched on the last few bricks of a long-forgotten wall, sometimes sprawled on the grass. At times, he poured water or wine over the fabric to create a feverish heat. An aftermath.

They complained of the cold, but hey, that's what happens when you pose essentially nude in New England in October. The way the cool air pinched their skin gave off the erotic vibe he'd hoped for—their nipples had hardened into delicate rose-buds. It was as if he'd controlled the temperature himself.

Jeff switched lenses. "I want you close together. Huddle for warmth. No, wait. Lesley, lay on your back with your legs spread open, your knees propped up. Mariana, straddle her. Kira, let one of the bra straps fall from your shoulder and kneel. Put Lesley's head in your lap."

They looked back at him blankly. *For fuck's sake, how hard could this be?* He went over and posed them like mannequins they were.

"Here." He bent Kira and Mariana over Lesley so that they resembled sexy wood nymphs. The dark, subtly gothic make-up accented those luscious mouths and big eyes well. He'd have to compliment his new go-to guy back in the city. Besides, he'd probably score another free bj.

He went to work clicking and whirring and moving their malleable parts swiftly, his cock twitching with every glimpse of secret, tender pink nook.

***

At first, he didn't see them.

Gray mist—in the middle of the day—sunk into a space be-tween one of the other ruins as if vacuumed down from below the earth. Another dark shadow, this one nearly opaque, materialized from thin air—hovered—and flitted into the invisible space where a wall once stood. While he stared at the eroded foundation, another shape—this one with clear wings—appeared in the distance behind a tree. It zipped across the open field and into the brush impossibly fast.

WHOMP! WHOMP! WHOMP! went the beating of the wings.

A prickling sweat began to creep up his chest and he stopped breathing. Jeff raised his camera and pressed the button down, setting off the shutter in rapid succession. He was aware of aiming the camera like a gun in self-defense.

A blurry black shape floated among the trees. Like the others, it didn't have a face or eyes. But unlike the other apparitions, he felt a rage emanating from it like heat evaporating from summer blacktop.

"Dude?" Kira asked.

Maybe he ought to get his eyes checked back home. At thirty-five, he shouldn't need to…but what the fuck was that?

He turned back to the models and rushed them through the rest of the shots—wine and sex be damned. He was no longer aroused. In fact, he felt even more chilled than the girls were.

**

"You're not staying overnight?" Laura Hickman, the Housatonic B&B proprietress asked, looking up from her book.

"Nope!" Jeff answered as he thundered down the stairs and slammed the key on the desk.

Laura frowned, standing from behind the check-in desk and her name plaque. "Oh, well, I can't give you a refund." She eyed the squirrely man and strangely made-up girls with wild manes. "Are you okay? Want some lemonade? Cookies?"

Jeff shot out the door, leaving the girls to scamper up to him. He barely waited until they were inside the Hummer before he stepped on the gas.

***

He drove in silence all the way back to New York. The girls had gotten used to his weird quietus, and he suspected they enjoyed it. They typed away on their phones or yammered to each other, comparing outfits, jobs, and stylists on this shoot or that. Jeff couldn't wait to be rid of them. He dropped them off at their agency and sped away as fast as he was able, given city traffic.

It wasn't until he'd clamped all five padlocks shut on his Williamsburg loft door that he exhaled. The familiar sights of his couch, expansive kitchen, and blown-up silver prints welcomed him. He flicked the light on. No shadows here. He crossed the room and collapsed onto the couch, setting the gear bags down on the floor. The unopened second bottle of wine beckoned, and he snatched the pinot noir from his pack, unscrewed, and arced it to his mouth in one motion. The smooth-yet-complex flavors brought him back to reality as the wine coursed over his tongue and down his throat.

Jeff flipped on the TV for a distraction, or at least, some background noise. Even so…he stared at the camera bag.

Could there be something in those photos? Something besides the girls?

He eyed the bag until he couldn't take it anymore, and snatched the camera out of it. With the wine bottle in the other hand, he was immersed in the comforting red darkroom lights in record time.

***

Unlike most modern photographers, Jeff didn't rely solely on digital media—he was an artist, damn it. He preferred real film, especially for large-format projects and gallery showings. He'd converted a large walk-in closet into a real darkroom upon moving into the loft, a luxury passed down from his Wall Street dad, who'd used the place as a getaway fuck palace when he didn't feel like being with his family—and that ended up being most days. As much as he'd resented the strife and turmoil back then, the large apartment had come in handy—especially since real estate had gone through the stratosphere. Unless you'd been born with money, were in organized crime, or had inherited property, owning anything in the city was highly unlikely and unaffordable for the working class.

As he waited for the developing solution to create images on the photo paper, he drank—and the bottle went fast. He sighed, knowing that this should have been consumed in Connecticut with three wispy waifs that could have so easily been taken advantage of… But there would be more—there were always more, either from Russia or Honduras or Norway or whatever. Everyone wanted to be a fucking star. What they didn't realize was the supreme amount of *getting* fucked you had to do to make that happen.

Hours dissolved as he processed every single exposure, itching to see…the beneath. Fuck the contact sheet; he was going to see everything materialized on 8x10" Illford paper. The chemicals and wine dizzied Jeff as he waited in the red light. Eventually, trees and limbs and girls appeared after several laborious washes in developer, stop-bath fluid, fixer, a final rinse, and a run in the print dryer.

***

Jeff spread the prints out on the huge worktable in his living room. He wasn't sure what he was supposed to find, or if he was ready to see the black shapes again. He shuffled the images.

Everything seemed normal. The decrepit foundations did look creepy behind the girls—out of place and unsettling—exactly the weird dichotomy he wanted to create with the models. However, there was nothing there that shouldn't have been.

A sigh escaped him that he didn't realize he was holding in. A trip to the eye doctor was in his immediate future—hell, an MRI, too. He rubbed his neck and almost smiled. How silly. Feeling a wave of exhaustion, he turned off the lights and collapsed into bed.

***

The sensation of being watched prompted Jeff to open his eyes. He turned away from the bright sun pouring in through the slats of the bedroom blinds.

Kira stood in the doorway, completely nude.

His body jerked, but he didn't cry out the way he wanted to. Why was he so terrified that a twelve-year-old girl was in his bedroom? It wasn't like it hadn't happened before.

"How did you get in?"

She didn't answer him. She just stood there and kept staring.

He sat up. "Kira?"

She seemed to come to life at the mention of her name, and nearly ran to him. Shoving him back down into the sheets, the girl ripped off his blanket and jumped on him. Overruled by the nagging in his boxers and the sudden onslaught of kisses, his fear subsided.

"Well good morning." It was rare that a model came after him. "Have fun yesterday?" She paused, watching him. And then she yanked off his shorts.

"Whoa!" After the shock of a feast handing itself to him subsided, he was aboard for the ride. "Okay, let's go." He grabbed her and flung her down easily—she couldn't have weighed more than a hundred pounds. Reversing their positions, he ground his hips into hers, bony and small as they were, and closed his eyes to take in the full effect of his other senses, to completely experience the delights of this new conquest.

Her mouth tasted sweet, the pillowy lips welcoming and pliant against his tongue. His arms snaked beneath her and tightened; if she had second thoughts about waking him, he wasn't going to let her get away now.

He kept kissing her, and when he was fully ready for the ride, he hiked up one of her legs. She tasted strange now, a little too floral, a little too sweet, and his stomach lurched.

Jeff opened his eyes and dry heaved.

Sunken, blackened pits filled with writhing white maggots had replaced her vibrant blue eyes. The skin around her sockets—and entire face—was rotten and peeling, her lips nearly gone, and her hair sparse, brittle, grayed and torn. Yellow, brackish putrescence poured from her mouth, splashing onto his face and into his sheets.

He screamed and launched himself backwards off the bed and the floor shot up and bludgeoned his head, sending a blinding cataclysm through his vision. His sight blinked white, and then black.

***

The ceiling swam. The pain in his skull knocked and knocked, waiting to be let out.

Then he remembered the corpse in his bed.

His blood quickened and he tried not to breathe…or imagine that thing. He sat up slowly, the edge of the mattress coming into view. The desiccated body was gone. He touched the soft cotton sheets with shaking fingers; they were clean and dry, unspoiled from any leaking thing. He quietly rose to his knees. Jeff was alone in the room. Sandpaper in his throat and on his tongue, he giggled just the same.

It's time to book a vacation.

Some place tropical where he could sip countless margaritas, swim, and shoot in a remote locale, maybe among the lesser-known cays of the Bahamas. He'd take along a girl or two who had absentee parents and ached for attention, sun, and new portfolio shots.

But first, a shower.

***

Settling into his cushy first-class seat, Jeff clicked on his seat belt and accepted a drink offer from the flight attendant. He'd scored an assignment for the new season's swimwear line from one of the world's top designers, and he was feeling flush. The agency's girls were already settled in Belize, and he'd learned that these girls were brand new to the industry—fresh discoveries that had wandered in for some test shots.

He accepted his gin and tonic from the attendant and sipped the cool drink down with a Xanax. Time for a well-deserved nap. As he drifted into sleep, he smiled at the thought of coconut-scented suntan oil and slippery skin and moist holes that he couldn't wait to get his hands on.

***

A lovely little girl sat on his lap, lips glossy pink and hair a perfect beachy mane as she rocked back and forth on his hardening member. Jesus Christ, what a dream this girl was. She giggled and sucked on a finger, making him moan.

"Goddamn, girl, you're gonna go far in this business." He lay back on the sand, tilted the camera up, and focused.

"Are you a virgin?" he couldn't help but ask.

She gave him a devilish grin and pulled at her top, showing more skin. "Not for long, Daddy."

"Holy shit," he groaned. He couldn't believe his luck. Pure, prime meat—his for the taking. If she was going to keep up like this, they'd have a long career together. She'd be a superstar, he'd make sure of it.

The sea lapped at his ankles as the sun set behind them. He clicked away as she bounced, giving him the sexiest shoot she could.

She couldn't have been more than twelve years old.

Jeff reached up and untied her string bikini top. It fell away. Caved-in holes where her nipples should have been. Huge hairy fists punched out of her chest and choked him as the roar of a jet screeched in his ears. He screamed, bucking up—

"Sir, are you okay? Sir, wake up!"

Drenched in sweat, he stopped flailing. "Would you like another drink? We're nearly to our destination."

His fellow first-class passengers were staring. Then he saw his erection attempting to break out of his pants and crossed his legs, sitting up. What an embarrassment. No more mixing Xanax with alcohol, then. But until next time—

"Yeah, gimme that drink, thanks," he swallowed.

***

The Belize shoot had been an absolute hit. It had filled his bank account as it had emptied his cock and everyone else had seemed to have a good time, too. Even the laughable chaperone the agency had sent down with the models had gotten some free drugs and a good pounding or four, courtesy of his never-ending vigor. Work was good—better than ever—and he thought about new shoot concepts for upcoming shoots, like gloriously seedy dungeon shoots, real S&M stuff.

Two months went by without further spectral provocation as he plundered and tasted the sweetness of more children.

Jeff had pushed the nightmares and incidents of Dudleytown—and the Kira apparition—out of his mind. His photographs were fine, showing no odd shapes, smears, or scratches either on the negatives or prints. The resulting fashion spread had been approved with accolades for a spring layout, and the prestigious David Price gallery in Chelsea was set to premiere his work.

In fact, the opening reception was in just a few hours. Jeff treated himself to a shave and borrowed a designer suit from one of his best clients, Peter Devensworth, who also happened to be the creator of the new lingerie line worn by "the girls who got away," as he liked to think of them. Ah well, there were always others, an infinite parade of fresh young bodies thrown to him in the most fashionable gristle mill ever.

The polished Oxfords Jeff wore were a gift, courtesy of the same guy and his budding footwear line. Jeff couldn't wait to shoot girls wearing nothing but heels, slippers, sandals, wedges…it was going to be good. And after the fall show at Bryant Park, he knew that Devensworth would have a party with a secret room, like he always did. Within that hideaway, young, eager-to-please preteen models would be hired as wait staff to serve them. It'd be a Roman orgy of epic proportions.

***

"Jeff!" He looked up as he entered the gallery. David Price smiled and waved him over. He took a glass of champagne from a wandering waiter and approached.

"Welcome back! There are a few people I want to introduce you to, including the new owner of your largest portrait!"

Jeff couldn't help but grin. The huge silver gelatin print surely cost a pretty price, netting a windfall for both himself and the gallery. The photo in question was the centerpiece of the collection; it hung high on chic gray walls above gleaming hardwood floors scented faintly with lemon oil.

The image of Kira, Mariana, and Lesley and their long limbs—entangled in sheer lingerie and matching, flowing sashes—dominated the room. It was arousing yet artful, perfect for a connoisseur of any taste—or for a simple admirer of beauty. The deep saturated greens and blues contrasted with the sheer white fabric stretched across skin had been captivating in his studio. Now that it was framed, the image was quite haunting.

"You've really outdone yourself, Jeff," Price murmured. "It was sold before I even opened the doors today."

"Really?"

Price nodded. "I have a few high net-worth clients who are worth letting in early, especially for forty grand. That's before my commission, of course."

Jeff grinned. "Well then, I'll have to do another shoot!"

Price laughed and clapped him on the back in a half-hug. "Oh, I think so! Let me find our patron after I powder my nose." He made a loud sniffing sound and winked as he walked away.

Jeff smiled again and turned back to—

The faces. The girls' faces were withered, the skin torn showing impossible red tissue beneath, the eye sockets sunk and black, their dried lips curled back over yellowed, broken teeth and hissing hissing HISSING cutting through the din of the crowd, the sound of beating, leathery wings coming closer—

The angry mocking tinkle of his champagne glass shattering on the floor broke his gaze.

As the well-dressed crowd turned to gape at him, a flurry of wait staff rushed his way, pulling out pristine white towels, cleaning, asking if he was all right.

No way was he all fucking right.

He glanced back at the photo. It was perfectly fine. Jeff's guts twisted and he muttered an "excuse me" to no one in particular and rushed to the bathroom. He turned the faucet and splashed his face with cold water, hoping to douse away the heat and sweat coming from his pores.

He looked at his reflection in the mirror. Other than a freaked out face, he looked normal. Maybe he should go home, to be safe. He'd put in an appearance. He could just tell Price that he thought he was getting food poisoning or something.

***

Other than a few sideways glances, no one paid him much mind as he scurried back into the gallery. Unable to *not* look at the photo, Jeff stole a peek, relieved to find that the horrible visages were gone.

He turned to take off and leave the whole affair behind him, but nearly ran into Price. "Hey, look who I found! Jeff, this is Werner Elser, industrialist and an admirer of your work. He's the one who bought your centerpiece."

"God help you," he muttered.

Surprise painted the distinguished German elder's face.

"Vat?"

A shadow caught his eye, and his heart shuddered. Coal black spots bled out from the eyes of the models in the image—all three of them—not stopping and coming out of their mouths and noses, and poured down the print and dripped to the floor becoming a puddle then a shape that started sliding across the shining wood toward him. The puddle-shape rose into the air and grew wings, drifting even closer until it was just over the heads of his patrons.

WHOMP. WHOMP. WHOMP.

The beating of the wings snuffed out the sound of his racing heart.

He heard himself making terrified, mewling sounds. The thing wouldn't stop coming.

"Do you see it?! DO YOU SEE?!" he screamed.

The alarmed men looked around, confused.

Price grabbed his arms. "What's this, what are you going on about? See what?" He hushed at Jeff as he struggled in his grasp. "Stop!"

The thing slid closer and he yanked away from the gallery owner's grip and pointed.

We see you.

The voice in his head wasn't one, but an army—and none of them, speaking together, sounded human.

The shape picked up speed and Jeff shrieked and fled the gallery.

***

He slammed the loft's door shut and cranked every padlock before sliding to the floor as tears spilled down his cheeks. Maybe he'd finally cracked after too many drugs, too much alcohol, too much seed spent.

A zap of freezing cold shocked his hand and he leapt from the spot.

The black shape pooled toward him from beneath the door.

A bright FLASH and a shutter whirring in concert—opening and closing in rapid staccato.

"Fuck!!" He covered his eyes enough to fend off most of the light, but... His camera was going off by itself from the table, producing a strobe effect in the dark. Across the room, the bulb flash felt like invisible fists of white heat pounding his sight into KOs.

Whispers in a language he did not understand came from the direction of the door. They got louder, rising to a frenzied crescendo inside his brain until he covered his ears and squeezed his eyes shut, screaming and kicking at the air.

Jeff opened his eyes, stunned to find himself back in the Dudleytown clearing.

Several figures floated above him; they were still dark as night and had taken the form of something like people, but not quite. Although he could not see their eyes, he saw the smudged edges of their forms—Jesus, those huge black wings—and felt their stares burning his skin, judging him, and he was transfixed. Prickles of ice crept across him until he was sure he was about to drown in a frozen lake that existed in some invisible dimension between this world and the next.

A deafening growl punched out his hearing as a putrid wind filled his nostrils and gagged him, as if winged demon hounds now carried him to Hell—roaring pressure carrying him down, ripping him from Earth. An unseen force crushed his chest with a brutal weight, sucking the air from him. His ribs cracked and pierced his lungs. He tried to scream, but his own blood began the slow, agonizing process of drowning him. Quiet settled, but only for a moment. The far-off wail of a woman echoed throughout the abandoned settlement. Screams of children followed, rising in pitch and building until the weight of the combined volume forced blood to explode from his eardrums.

When they found what was left of his body after three weeks of decomposition, the juices he left puddled on the loft floor resembled the dark shapes that had hunted him.

WILDERNESS

BY LETITIA TRENT

The airport was small, squat like a compound, its walls interrupted in regular intervals by tall, shaded windows. When Krista looked out the windows, the sky seemed slate-gray and heavy, but when the front doors opened, she remembered that it was really blue and cloudless outside.

She was early for her flight back to New Haven. She liked to arrive at the very earliest time the flight website recommended. She was prepared to wait, liked it even. It was calming to have nothing to do and nowhere she had to be. She had brought a book about the history of wilderness and America, something left over from college that she had never read. She liked the cover, a picture of a Pilgrim family, small and sickly, their clothes black and heavy on their bony bodies, facing an expanse of trees so tall and green you could see nothing beyond them. She underlined phrases in the book out of old college habit: Wilderness remained a place of evil and spiritual catharsis. Any place in which a person feels stripped, lost, or perplexed, might be called a wilderness.

She shared a red, plush armrest with a large woman who had almost incandescent, butter-blonde hair. Her skin was so tan that it reminded Krista of a stain. Coffee on blonde wood.

The blonde had apparently just come from a trip to Maine. She told an older woman next to her—an even larger woman with tight pin-curls and wire-rimmed glasses, wearing those boxy, pleated shorts that middle-aged women often wear on holidays—about her trip. The blonde had stayed in the cutest hotel. Her entire room had been done up all nautical. The other woman nodded in agreement with everything the blonde said, as if she had had an identical experience.

Krista watched the airport attendants and one airport policeman patrol the area. They sometimes stepped into the waiting room and observed the crowd with what appeared to be either worry or constipation (they pressed their lips together, their hands on their hips, and blew the air from their mouths as if making silent raspberries). They had a vague air of agitation. She watched them carefully for signs of what might be wrong, but they revealed nothing in their pacing. Nobody else seemed to notice.

On Krista's left, opposite the blonde, was a family, a mother and two children separated from her by one seat. The mother was thin and loud and wore shorts with many utilitarian pockets and a simple tank shirt without a bra. She seemed infinitely capable, as if she ran her own business or perhaps even managed some kind of sports team. Krista admired thin, efficient women like this, women who wore comfortable, rubber-soled sandals and clothing with enough functional pockets. The woman and her children all spoke on their individual cell phones, all telling somebody variations on the news that they would arrive soon, that it was only thirty minutes until boarding.

An announcement crackled over the loudspeakers, the sound delivered in one chunk of indiscernible static.

Krista looked around the room, hoping for the scraps of

somebody else's conversation to explain what had just been said.

Plane's delayed for an hour, the blonde said to her husband, who had also missed it. Storms down in Boston.

A general grumble rose. People shifted in their seats and took out their recently stowed cell phones. The blonde woman called her husband's name, which Krista immediately forgot.

Phone me up a pizza, she told him. I won't eat that shit from the vending machine.

***

As it grew darker in the waiting room, Krista struggled to make out the print of her book. The primary row of fluorescent lights hadn't been turned on, but nobody else had complained about the dark yet. She wouldn't be the first. She read until she had to squint in the darkness at the small, cramped words.

As she tried to concentrate on the increasingly turgid prose of her book (pages and pages about national forests, conservationists, things that Krista wasn't particularly interested in, though she knew that she should be), the blonde woman spoke energetically about her two dachshunds, Buckeye and Alexis. They liked to eat the carpet, she said, so she had soaked the edges of the carpet in Tabasco sauce, which was, incidentally, the same color as the carpet. The pin-curled woman asked how they managed to walk on the carpet if it was soaked with Tabasco sauce. The blonde shrugged, as if this were a mystery to her as well, though a boring one that she had no interest in pursuing.

Krista gave up on her book.

The mother and her children slept on the carpet below their chairs, their bookbags slung up on the seats above them, the fabric of their bulky Plymouth Rock sweatshirts bunched under their heads as pillows.

Krista wished that she could step outside and occupy herself with a cell phone, as many others did, but she didn't have a cell phone (she had canceled it when she'd left her job) and had nobody to call. Nobody was waiting to meet her in New Haven, and nobody was worried that her flight was late. She stood up and let the cheese cracker crumbs gathered in the folds of her T-shirt fall to the carpet.

***

Krista stood in the fluorescent lights of the bathroom, listening for shuffling feet, a toilet paper roll spinning. She was alone. Her stall door wouldn't shut completely (how did doors come unlined from their frames? She didn't understand what would cause it, other than a fundamental shifting of the floor), so she kept one hand on the door as she pulled down her underwear. A bumper sticker on the inside of the door said Republicans for Voldemort. She had never seen a Harry Potter movie or read one of the books, but she vaguely knew who Voldemort was. She was in on the joke.

She put her hand on the sticker and tried to keep the door closed as she eased her jeans and underwear down. It was just as she'd thought—in the middle of the bone-colored strip of fabric, a slight red stain. She peeked out her door into the empty bathroom: no machines.

Krista stuffed a ball of toilet paper between her legs and pulled her pants back up, letting the door open slightly, as she needed both hands. As she did this, just as the door swung open and she saw a middle-aged woman in the bathroom mirror carefully applying liquid eyeliner, the bathroom lights cut out. Nothing hummed or whirred and she could hear people in the hallway shuffling and speaking.

She buttoned her pants in the darkness and stepped into the bathroom, lit only by the dusky light seeping through the high, small window above the sinks. The woman applying eyeliner hissed shit and left, slamming her purse or hip into the plastic trash barrel as she left.

Before Krista even had time to panic or feel anything but mild interest, the electricity came back on again. The fluorescents above her buzzed with the effort and her blue-lit face appeared in the mirror. She was alone again. She washed her hands and pressed her wet palms over her face.

***

Ladies and gentlemen, a police officer said, shaking the flashlight in his hand in time with the syllables, sorry for the inconvenience. He and one of the nervous attendants stood before the check-in desk.

It's only a temporary outage, the officer assured them. Nothing serious.

Krista made her way back to the waiting room, stepping over legs and bookbags.

The news drifted into the main room, where Krista's jacket was twisted around one leg of her chair, her carry-on bag placed on her seat to save it. The blonde next to her watched the progress of her bag as she removed it and sat down again. She knew that she shouldn't leave her bags unattended—signs on every wall said so in bold, red letters. All she had in the bag were dirty clothes, a brochure about Maine blueberries that her mother had given her, and a business card from her father's company with a telephone number scrawled on the back. Nothing she was afraid of losing.

Her parents wanted her to come back home to Maine. She hadn't told them yet that she wouldn't. She was jobless now, that was true, but it wasn't as they feared—she wasn't beyond help. She had skills. She imagined herself combing through the classifieds in a coffee shop, circling job after job, making cheerful telephone inquiries, putting more action words in her résumé (implemented, facilitated, utilized). The idea didn't scare her. It seemed liberating. Fun, even. She remembered several cheerful montages from romantic comedies that included these very scenes. They had to have happened to somebody.

Did you hear what he said back there? The blonde demanded. It was a rhetorical question, since she obviously knew. Krista nodded and told her anyway.

So what's the problem? The blonde asked. She was suspicious, if not of Krista, then at least of the policeman's words.

Storms. Storms are the problem, Krista repeated.

The woman sniffed and shook her head, kicking off her pink flip-flops. Storms. I bet.

***

It was completely dark out now. Somebody had put the lights on in the main room, so Krista could no longer see the parking lot and tree-heavy outskirts from the window. The pizza delivery car had taken forty-five minutes to reach the airport. He had reported heavy wind and rain somewhere close and coming toward them. The woman and her husband ate an entire large pizza all by themselves. Krista didn't want any of their pizza, but she found it rude for people to eat in the presence of others who were not eating.

She couldn't concentrate on her book. She put it away and

tucked her luggage under her seat. She stood up, feeling the blood rush back into her legs. She'd go outside—the air in here was stuffy, full of the smells of powdered cheese and industrial cleaning liquid.

The glass doors folded away instantly for her, as if she had bid them to do so.

Outside it was still, but the streets were slick, as if it had recently rained, though she had seen no rain. A group of men stood by the doorway, talking about a sports team that she didn't know.

He could really fucking get that ball across the field, he said. That boy was something else. This was from an airport attendant, one she had not seen before, a young man with a slightly fat, womanish body—large hips and a round ass. The other men nodded in unison. They made brief eye contact with Krista and nodded in turn, as if she were a visiting dignitary, somebody who needed at least a modicum of acknowledgment. She smiled and looked down, the proper response.

The streetlights reflected back against the cloud-covered sky, giving it a uniform orangey, sick tinge. Shallow puddles of water collected at the edges of the lot. The entire parking lot was lit by rows and rows of light.

Out beyond the parking lot, Krista saw a paved footpath from the airport to a big, empty industrial complex next door. The flight, according to her blonde neighbor, was delayed for another hour. She had time for a walk.

She set off across the lot, hoping that the men on the steps were watching. She didn't want to be stranded if the plane happened to arrive early and everybody boarded without her. She imagined coming back to find the waiting room empty, her piece of luggage the only sign left that the place had once been inhabited.

The air was humid but cool. A cold sweat gathered on her bare throat and forehead as she pumped her arms and walked fast to reach the walkway. She wanted to be far away from the airport, to be able to see it from a distance. As a child, she had often fantasized about opening the car door and just running into the woods that lined the highways in Maine, disappearing from her parents and never arriving at whatever place they'd intended to take her. She often had a desire for literal distance from places, to see them in perspective to the sky or horizon. It calmed her to see something that made her afraid or unhappy small against a forest or cloudbank.

She crossed the wooded median and broke through to the parking lot of the complex. She turned around. The airport looked small in comparison to the huge building next to her, which had at least a dozen stories and was completely made of glass.

A light swiveled continually from the airport's roof. From a distance, she could see the people inside the building below the fluorescent lights. The blonde chewed a piece of crust. One of the men outside lit a cigarette. The match flamed in his hands and then disappeared. She sat down on a bench facing the airport, and then rested her head on the slats. She was tired, she realized, and the swampy air increased the feeling. She would only close her eyes for a while.

***

Ma'am. Ma'am! The voice woke Krista immediately. A flashlight bobbed around her face. She tried to speak, but only a low moan came out.

Are you hurt? Are you all right, Ma'am? The policeman (Krista could see his badge and recognized his slick black hair from the airport) flashed his light into her eyes. She sneezed, then sat up, wiping her nose on the back of her hand.

I'm fine, she said. Is something the matter?

The policeman stood up from his crouching position. He towered over her as she sat, stood too close. Her nose was level with the brass button on his pants. She stood up.

I'm supposed to get everybody back to the airport. Storm coming. The flight is delayed for another hour. He jerked his head toward the airport. The men over there said you'd walked out thisaway and I came to get you. The policeman turned and started back toward the airport, so Krista followed.

I'm sorry to trouble you, she said to his back. She hadn't imagined somebody would come to get her—why would he do that? Had he been watching her?

His shoulders were very broad. She liked how every policeman called every woman Ma'am, even if the woman was clearly younger than he was.

The policemen shook his head. No trouble. He didn't turn to look at her.

Krista wondered when the storm would come. The sky was still a strange, flat, orange-black.

***

When Krista entered the room, the blonde woman and her husband looked away.

Found the last one, the policeman announced to the airport attendant.

Go ahead and take a seat, he told her.

It seemed to her that the whole room watched as she walked to her seat, removed her luggage, and sat down. Some of them didn't take their eyes from her even as the airport attendant began to speak. She looked at the floor.

It looks like we'll be keeping you for another hour, ladies and gentlemen, he said. The airport attendant looked around the room nervously, his hand rested on the top of his walkie-talkie. He wanted to leave, Krista could tell. He placed one foot behind him, ready to pivot him away. The flight is having minor technical difficulties, which should be resolved within the hour. He took a breath. But we got one request from the local authorities—you all must stay inside until the airplane lands.

At the word authorities, the room's temperature changed. The blonde's husband sat up straight in his seat and began to protest, as did several other men. The children looked at their mothers. The mothers pulled their children close.

What authorities, exactly? A few voices asked, stepping closer to the front counter.

Krista watched the airport attendant's face. He put his hand up and grimaced. I don't have any information beyond what I have given you.

Safe from what? What kind of danger, exactly, might we be in? A balding man in khaki pants stepped forward. He stood with two children—a boy and a girl of seemingly equal age, both thin and uncannily poised, their hair long and neat and pulled away from their faces. They looked just like him, tall and thin with large, bony elbows and hands.

The attendant shook his head. Sir, I only know what I've been told. All I know is that you are not in any immediate danger, as long as you stay in the airport.

Krista felt her stomach pang. She'd been outside. Was she in danger? Or was it only right now that the outdoors was dangerous? She turned and tried to see outside the windows, but she could only see the reflection of the group on the glass.

Listen, another man said, we need to know—but the attendant's walkie-talkie crackled and he held his hand up, pressing it against his face. He spoke into it, a series of yeses and nos. The attendant held up one finger to the crowd, indicating just a minute, and returned to the gated doors that separated the waiting room from the security check.

When he left, people looked around, dazed. Some began to speak to each other, to people they would not otherwise speak to. Fear, Krista saw, made them trust each other with their own fear. They turned to each other and said plainly I am afraid. Not in those words, but in other words and in the angles of their bodies, in how much closer they leaned, how much more quickly they spoke.

The skinny mother with many-pocketed pants called hey, hey in Krista's direction, and she gradually realized that the woman was speaking to her.

Did you see anything while you were outside?

Krista felt the attention of the room turned to her.

She shook her head. Nothing. I didn't see anything. It was completely calm.

The blonde's husband snorted. Calm, he repeated. Krista looked at him, not sure what he meant. Did he think she was lying?

Did you see any people out there? The woman asked, her eyes darting around Krista's head.

No, nobody but the policeman. Krista didn't like the way they watched her. Their eyes narrowed as if they couldn't quite get her into focus.

***

The police arrived thirty minutes later. She could see their squad cars' headlights momentarily illuminate the otherwise black parking lot. They did not have their sirens on, but when they emerged from the squad cars, they were wearing masks. It was difficult to see exactly what kind of masks (she had only the light from their headlights to see by), but they seemed to be gas masks—a thick tube like an elephant tusk hung down from each policeman's mouth and nose.

One of the children said His mask is scary. He pointed, and they all looked out the window, some running up to press their hands and faces to the glass. The entire window was covered with people trying to see through it. Krista remained seated. She'd seen the masks and didn't know how it would help to see more. She could also feel that she was bleeding and was afraid to stand up.

Fuck this, said a young man, one of the people pressed against the glass. He was handsome in a slim, well-groomed way that made Krista nervous. Men like this didn't notice her unless she was doing something for them—putting their call through at her office, for instance (her former office, she reminded herself), or reminding them to sign a form. They might reply thank you, while looking right through her. This man was dark-haired and wore a T-shirt of a solid, rich color—a brownish brick. He looked as if he'd stepped from an Eddie Bauer catalog. Krista's mother got an Eddie Bauer catalog every month. She remembered admiring those outdoorsy people, thirtysomething, financially stable, wearing primary colors and sturdy shoes. They had formed her idea of what it meant to be a happy adult.

I'm going to see what's going on here, he told the room. People around him nodded, even the mothers, who Krista thought might be offended by the fact that he had just said fuck, but maybe they excused the language in an emergency situation.

The man walked up to the glass accordion doors. Before, they had immediately opened when anyone stepped close to them.

Now, they didn't open. They must have cut the power to the doors. For the first time that night, she began to understand why everybody else was so frightened. It had taken her longer, she thought, because she only had herself to be afraid for.

The Eddie Bauer man pounded lightly on the glass doors, which shook under his fists. They were not very solid. He could have broken them if he wanted to.

Give us some fucking information! He screamed at the plastic seal in the middle of the door. Krista had an urge to laugh, but she turned it into a cough. She didn't want to offend the man, who had done nothing to warrant unkindness.

It must be chemicals. Some kind of chemicals outside, the blonde said. Then she repeated it, looking around the room for somebody to tell. It must be chemicals. We've been attacked with chemicals and we're stuck here. Her husband nodded.

Some of the men, older ones with children, went to look for the airport attendant and the policeman, who had all disappeared during the half hour before the police in gas masks had arrived.

Did you smell any gas out there? The blonde turned to Krista. This is important. Did you smell anything?

She wanted to help the woman. She tried to remember smells. The hedges smelled like pine. The bed of flowers around the industrial complex smelled like fresh manure and maple syrup.

No, I didn't smell anything unusual. Krista shifted in her seat and felt her stomach heave and salt at the back of her throat. She was going to be sick. But she couldn't be sick here, not with then all looking at her, thinking she'd been poisoned.

The blonde shook her head and turned from Krista, done with her. I don't want to die in the goddamn place. I don't want to die. Her husband gathered her in his arms and pulled her away from Krista. He shot her a look of mild anger, as if it were her fault that the woman was upset.

Krista stood up, hoping to leave the room for a while, to go to the bathroom and rest her cheek against the cool stall door and be away from the constant noise, the questions.

Mommy! A girl raced down the hallway, almost colliding with Krista as she ran. Mommy, the water hurt me! The little girl's mouth was red with blood. It smeared her lips like lipstick. At first Krista thought it was lipstick, but it was wet on her hands, too, which she held out before her.

What did you do, baby? What happened? This wasn't the many-pocketed mother, but a more frantic mother, one who wore a jumper and a headband. She was as upset as the child.

What hurt you, baby?

Krista stood in the hallway watching, like everyone else, waiting to hear what was wrong. She stood perfectly still, afraid that moving would collide her with whatever had hurt the child. The child sniffled and hiccupped, but eventually, she managed to get something out. She had only taken a drink from the water fountain. It had cut her, and she had come back here to tell her mother about it.

As the mother wiped the child's mouth clean with a napkin from her purse, they heard a rustle from the front of the room—the security door opened and the attendant stepped out, his walkie-talkie crackling.

Good, you're all here, the airport attendant said, surveying the group. He did not seem to notice that they were gathered together strangely, turned toward the mother and child in the middle.

You might have noticed the police presence, he said. They are here to secure the airport. He held up his hand when somebody spoke, the tone angry, though they were not able to get out a word. The plane is scheduled to leave in thirty minutes, it has just landed. We've put a plastic tunnel from the door to the plane so you don't have to go outside when you board, just as a precaution—understand? He paused and looked at the bulky, digital face of his watch.

The blonde jumped in, ignoring his still-raised hand. What's going on? Have we been attacked? She held a paper towel to her eyes and dabbed beneath them where her eyeliner bled.

The attendant shook his head. No Ma'am, no evidence of that. The FBI determines that. You'll know as soon as I know. The man nodded at them all, and, as the questions began, as the mother with the bloody-mouthed child tried to bring the child forward, a paper-towel held against the girl's still lips, the man walked fast—almost jogged—back to the gated security area, slid through the smallest possible sliver of open door, and then locked the door behind him.

The crowd was still for what seemed like a very long time to Krista, though she knew it was probably only a few seconds. Then, the Eddie Bauer man ran up the slight slope to the locked entrance and shook the gate like somebody in a prison movie or a primate behind old-fashioned zoo bars.

We've got a kid bleeding in here. We want to speak to somebody in charge. His voice echoed in the empty security area and bounced back down to the crowd.

The mother held her daughter and began to cry. The child was dry-eyed. Everyone was speaking but Krista. Unlike the others, she was uncoupled, without a child or a traveling companion. In Victorian novels, women always went with traveling companions, maiden aunts or cousins to keep them safe from the influence of crowds and sinister men. They also served another purpose, one which Krista had not thought of before—they were for company, somebody to be with, a buffer against loneliness beyond the everyday loneliness of being in one's own head. She usually enjoyed her own company, but her aloneness oppressed her here. Even now, people did not usually travel alone, at least not the way she was, aimlessly and with nowhere to go, no one to care if she arrived or not.

She imagined that the others sometimes looked at her sideways, never directly. Krista wasn't sure if she was exaggerating their glances—her mother said that she tended to suspect dislike where it wasn't present. You were always a fussy, fearful child, she'd said during her latest visit, after Krista had explained what had happened at her job, with her boss, how she had been shamed into leaving, how he had never called her again. I'm sure it would have blown over if you'd just waited. If you'd just been a little more goddamn calm about it.

Being fearful makes people want to hurt you, her mother had said. When you shrink away, people want to give you a reason to shrink.

Krista tried to breathe deeply to calm herself. She opened her bag and took out her book. She had read only one half-sentence (Wild animals added danger to the American wilderness and here, too, the element of the unknown intensified feelings) before she felt her stomach tighten. She had the urge to stretch out on the floor until the sickness passed, but she couldn't. She put her book away and rose. As she stood up, the blonde, now sitting with her head between her hands, the empty pizza box occupying the seat next to her, turned to watch.

Are you sick or something? The woman looked at Krista, though she kept her head in her hands.

I'm okay, Krista said. Just had too much water.

Her mother had always called her period her monthly friend, and Krista had been encouraged to adopt similar euphemisms for bodily functions. Going number two. Making water. Making wind. She couldn't imagine answering the woman's question truthfully.

The woman pursed her lips and nodded, but turned to Krista again, her face still blank. Sure you didn't pick up something from outside? You went farther out than any of us. As she said this, the woman weeping on her bleeding child's blonde head looked up.

Did you drink out of the water fountain? Did you get something from outside on the fountain?

Krista shook her head, rising again. No, no. I have my own water. I swear, there's nothing wrong with me. Nothing was wrong outside when I was out there. She looked at the two women, both staring at her, their mouths hardened, their teeth not showing.

Excuse me, she told them, as if ducking away from a dinner party. I have to use the restroom.

***

In the bathroom, Krista leaned her warm forehead against the bathroom stall, then thought better of it and pulled away. She didn't know it was safe to touch. Maybe she was getting poison on everything she touched. The woman's fear was convincing.

In the stall, she knelt and rested her head in her hands. Her head ached dully. She couldn't take one of the Tylenol she'd brought in her carry-on bags—she didn't have any water left in her bottle. She knelt until the sickness passed. But she had to go back. She couldn't hide.

Before she left the bathroom, she caught a flash of light in the small window above her eye level. They were just outside, the men in masks. Krista wondered if she could see anything— maybe something she could tell the others about, gain their favor with—through the small, rectangular window in the bathroom. She turned over the bathroom's metal trash can and climbed on it, holding the wall for balance, until she could see outside.

The window looked out into the front lawn of the airport. She saw three figures in jumpsuits gliding their flashlights along the lawn. One seemed to be examining the grass. Another seemed to be looking at the edge of the building, where the foundation met the ground. Another was farther off, sweeping his light in the little stand of trees between the airport and the industrial complex. Their motions seemed cursory, almost mocking, as if they were only putting on a show of searching, and not even a very convincing one.

Looking for someone you know? A man's voice surprised her, and Krista turned on the trash can, almost falling. It was the blonde's husband. He wasn't wearing his baseball cap and his reddish, curly hair was flat and greasy against his head like a stack of smashed bread.

You scared me, she said, not sure how to understand the man's presence in the women's room. Is something wrong with the men's room?

The man shook his head. I just came to make sure you were all right. You were taking so long. His voice was wrong; it didn't match his words. He smiled at Krista and motioned for her to join him.

Come on back out here. We've all got some questions.

Krista nodded, though she didn't understand what he was saying. Questions for her? When she entered the waiting room, she saw that her baggage had been opened. The Eddie Bauer man had her book in his hands. He wore rubber gloves (Krista wondered where he had gotten them—did he pack rubber gloves whenever he traveled?).

What are you doing?

The people around him looked up at her. They had all let

him do this, she could see. They all approved.

We found this, the blonde said, pointing at Krista's seat. The red seat was stained black in a neat, tea saucer-sized circle. You're bleeding. Why didn't you tell us?

They think I'm sick, she thought. It isn't— she began, but the woman with the many pockets interrupted her.

You haven't spoken, and you're traveling here alone, he said. You go outside right before the attack. You visit the restroom five or six times after. You don't call anyone to let them know what happened. You don't ask any questions, and you don't seem to be fazed by what's happening here. The woman held her hands up, palms to the sky. What are we supposed to think?

Listening to the woman, Krista almost felt convinced of her own suspicious behavior. She was vaguely afraid that they would find her out. But there's nothing to find, she soothed herself, there's nothing wrong with me. I'm only alone. There's nothing wrong with that.

You can't do this to me, she said instead, the words surprising her. How dare you do this to me? The words seemed familiar, like something she had seen on television, and they made her feel powerful. She wanted to hit the Eddie Bauer man and take her book back. She wanted to make the blonde stop smiling or smirking or whatever she was doing with her mouth.

What, do you think you are some kind of important person? That you're better than the rest of us? This was from the blonde. She crossed her arms over her chest. Krista imagined that this was the way she stood when scolding her children.

I am important, she told them, not sure what she was trying to say. Tell them about your monthly friend, she told herself and almost laughed out loud. I'm as important as—

She stopped when the lights went out. A few of the children screamed and the mothers hissed words of comfort. Krista didn't move. It seemed safer to stay where she was. No need to drag it out. No need to make things harder on everyone. Though it was dark, she could hear the rustle of someone moving toward her.

THE SILK ANGEL

CHRISTINE MORGAN

"**R**eady, kid?"

"Ready, sir."

Captain Hollister grinned and clapped Augustus on the back, hard enough to stagger him in his boots. "All right, then. In you go!"

"Yes, sir!" Augustus snapped a sharp salute.

He was hard-pressed to keep from grinning himself, and didn't begrudge in the least being addressed as 'kid.' True, most of the others weren't that much older than him, but in wartime the years between practically-sixteen and seventeen-through-nineteen could be ages.

Hard-won experience made men of boys. It gave them valor and glory, the pride to hold their heads high, having lain their lives on the line. For King and Country.

How any red-blooded chap could expect to show his face back home if he hadn't done his part...

Well, it would not be said of Augustus Arthur Michael Pearce!

With eager speed and nimble grace, he scrambled into the sturdy wicker basket. The addition of his slight weight—he was a lean, wiry youth—hardly made it sway at its moorings. Not when he'd be sharing the cramped quarters with the captain as well as the bulky equipment. Camera, radio, binoculars, the usual kit and canteen, maps and charts, everything they'd need.

Overhead, the balloon bobbed in the breeze, a great oblong cloth sausage-casing stuffed with hydrogen gas. A steel cable tethered it to a winch. The rest of the crew stood ready to loose it up, and reel it back in at the end of the observation session.

Augustus affixed the safety lines to his waist-harness and crowded himself into the corner to make room for Captain Hollister to swing a leg in.

"Tally-ho," the captain said, buckling his own. "The blue skies await! Launch us aloft, boys!"

The blue skies, Augustus decided not to point out, were rather less than exactly blue. They were, in fact, overcast with clouds, against which the various thin spirals of smoke from the battlefields blended into a grey haze. But it was a small matter, meaningless in the otherwise grander excitement of his first official mission.

That he had lucked into this—!

Not to say that he'd protest doing anything else, to be sure. Artillery, the front, even the trenches if need be. Whatever he could do. However he could best serve.

He gripped the basket's edge, eyes wide, the grin escaping. The winch creaked, the cable unspooled, and up they went with a giddy sensation of lift-and-rise. His stomach seemed to do a not-unpleasant flip as the ground dropped away.

The perspective...their own guardian anti-aircraft guns... tents and lorries, men scurrying about in diminishing size... the broadening expanse of countryside...the landscape a patchwork of farms and pastures...to one side, the glimmering ribbon of a river curling toward the roofs of a quaint little village... to the other, the churned and muddy smear of no-man's-land, pocked with foxholes, twisted with snarls of barbed wire…beyond that…

Beyond that, the enemy.

Everything looked so small, so far-away and fragile!

"Four thousand feet, kid, how do you like it?" Captain Hollister asked.

A delighted laugh was the best reply Augustus could give, staring agog in thrilled wonder at the panorama. Hollister laughed as well. He delivered another hearty back-clap that could have toppled the youth out of the basket if he hadn't been braced and holding on.

The grey clouds remained as distant as ever. Between clouds and land, planes swooped. Their own fighter aircraft patrolled nearby, in case any of the German pilots decided to take a chance at joining the roster of aces known as 'balloon busters.'

"Keep a particular eye out for that black-winged bastard," the captain added, a grimmer note entering his voice.

That black-winged bastard, as Augustus and everyone else in their regiment knew, was Oskar Luffengraf, who flew the Sturmvogel and had been responsible for the fiery, crashing, bullet-riddled deaths of far too many of their fellow balloonists.

"Yes, sir."

They went to work spotting for troop movements and artillery emplacements, relaying their findings to the lads below. It had to be quick work, because nothing got Fritz stirred into action like the sight of a balloon heading on high to have a looksie at what they were up to over there.

Soon enough, the Germans made their move. Engines snarled as they hove into view, dark silhouettes swarming against the grey. A squadron rose to meet them. Guns chattered and chuddered. Their propellers made circular, whirring blurs at their noses.

Augustus had seen aerial dogfights before, but always from terra firma. Never from up here, in their very midst as it were! Never as they wheeled and dived...as clusters of bullet-holes popped open like shocked eyes...as flames seethed and smoke spewed...as a plane corkscrewed down in a terrible dying spiral...as a man jerked, arms flailing, blood bursting from his shoulder in a spray...

He'd seen blood before, too. He'd seen men who'd been shot, and shelled, and shrapnel-torn. He'd seen men with limbs blown off by land mines. He'd seen men with their skin blistered, melting, sloughing off from exposure to lethal poison gas. He'd seen men kill and men die.

Now, up here, it occurred to him—as if for the first time, though he knew it wasn't—that he might have to kill. That he could be killed. That he could die.

Those pilots, those gunners and navigators, they were the cream of the crop, the best of the best, flying expensive planes that were the very pinnacle of modern warfare...and they were dying!

While he was a kid hanging under a balloon! A balloon! A bag of hydrogen, a bag that could be ruptured and explode into a fireball, plummeting thousands of feet to collapse in a blazing ruin!

A kid armed with a pocketknife, and a service revolver he'd never once fired at anything more dangerous than a big brown battlefield rat!

A kid who'd fibbed about his birthdate in order to enlist! Not because it would impress the girls—not just—and not just because it sounded so much more a grand adventure than sitting in school—not just—but because...patriotism, pride, King and Country!

His fingers clenched white-knuckled on the edge of the basket, the wicker pressing ridges into his palms.

"Get ahold of yourself, Artie," he said in an under-the-breath mutter, using the pet-name bestowed by a favorite cousin without even thinking. He dug deep and found the Pearce nerve, the Pearce backbone, the Pearce discipline of body and mind.

Captain Hollister, with steely aplomb, kept peering through his binoculars while shouting his observations into the phone. He paid no attention to the chattering gunfire, the soaring, banking planes, and the dull thunder of the anti-aircraft artillery.

"Sir!" Augustus cried. "The black-winged bastard, sir! The Sturmvogel!"

He pointed at the aircraft, painted black with white trim and jagged yellow stripes, each wing and the tail emblazoned with the image of a bird of prey, lightning bolts clutched sparking in its talons.

At that, the captain did turn. A snarl curled his lip. Though Augustus couldn't hear him over the din, he rather suspected he could guess the following utterance.

The Sturmvogel's guns flashed and spat, peppering their signature along the side of an olive-green biplane with white and red markings. Then a steel tube mounted on the German plane's outboard strut belched forth a rocket. It missed, veering a smoking trail past the balloon.

For one heart-stopping moment of clarity, Augustus saw the famed and hated Luffengraf, saw his square jaw and the tight line of his mouth, and the distinctive dueling scar that sliced across one cheekbone. He could not discern Luffengraf's eyes through the goggles but a chill prickled the nape of his neck and he knew their gazes, for that split-second, met.

And what, he wondered, did the flying ace see? A boy, just a kid, just a child? A boy as blond and blue-eyed as any German himself, as Luffengraf's own younger brother might be?

Or a Tommy, the enemy, hated and despised? One more face-less, nameless soldier? One more tally for his reaper's total, as he added another balloon to his record?

Luffengraf pulled the Sturmvogel into a steep climb. It roared, engines screaming, up and out of Augustus' sight.

"Take the charts!" Captain Hollister thrust the leather-bound and string-tied folio into his arms. "Tight to your chest!"

The men below at the winch were reeling them in, but it was much slower going, the balloon fighting the cable's insistent pull. Another German plane buzzed them, this one sporting the emblem of a war-axe wreathed in fire.

"Go!" The captain's back-slap was, this time, a deliberate shove. "Jump for it, kid!"

Augustus half-sprang, half-tumbled out of the basket. Sheer terror seized him, an instant of panic, as he fell into open space, still at least two thousand feet up. He felt a hitch at his harness where he'd affixed the shroud lines and briefly prayed that he had indeed affixed them correctly.

He wanted to squeeze his eyes shut but didn't dare. Instead, he looked frantically up at the canvas bag on the side of the basket, the bag to which the shroud lines led. His descent tugged the bag open. A wadded bundle dropped after him.

Then, out of nowhere, the Sturmvogel returned in a barrage of bullets. Wicker flew in shredded confetti. Sparks pinged from the equipment. Blood flew into the air again as Captain Hollister was driven backward in the disintegrating basket. The steel tube mounted on the plane's other wing coughed smoke.

The parachute unfolded with a pale, silken billow. As it blossomed out into a graceful dome, it obscured the rest of the scene above him from Augustus' view. But he didn't need to see to know that, this time, the incendiary rocket did not miss its mark.

***

Paul Ellory stood on a catwalk outside the manager's office, overlooking the main work-floor. He paused at the rail to rest, leaning on his cane. Cold, damp weather such as this pained his leg, badly broken in childhood and never properly healed.

It had kept him from the army. His mother always said that should make him thankful, as if a constant ache and stiff, clumsy gait were anything to be thankful for. Did it stop the pitying looks? Did it stop the sneering of the ladies of the White Feather brigade? As if he'd done it on purpose, perhaps. As if he'd been so prescient as to shatter his bones at the age of seven to avoid a war the likes of which no one—no one!—could possibly have foreseen?

He frowned, brows drawing together. Sarah, seeing this expression, evidently mistook it for a sign of disapproval, and scowled herself.

"I've done the best I could," she said. "I thought as you'd be pleased."

Brushing the bitter dregs of memory away, he turned to her and smoothed the frown into a smile. "I am, my dear. My mind wandered a moment. No. I am quite pleased. Quite. You've done very well."

Mollified, she likewise smoothed away the scowl and favored him with a smile of her own. He'd only just returned from months in London and abroad, entrusting the running and management of the factory to his capable wife.

Below them on the work-floor, under the harsh but yellowish glare of suspended lights, rows of large industrial sewing machines buzzed and droned like a busy hive. Women in plain dresses, their hair bound under kerchiefs or caps, fed piece after piece of pattern-cut cloth through them. The jabbing needles moved too fast for the eye to behold, stitching strong double-seams.

"And they're no trouble?" Paul asked. "The workers?"

Sarah shook her head. "No trouble at all. They're glad for the work. They have children at home, a lot of mouths to feed on scarce income. They need the money. As much as that, they're glad to have something to do, some way to feel useful and contribute to the cause."

There was, these days, a shortage of able-bodied grown men across much of England. Paul had only seen a handful of beardless youths and bearded elders in New Fairchurch, and a scattering of the unfit and the idiotic and mad. The rest had enlisted to fight the dirty Hun. They left behind their wives and sisters, daughters and mothers, households needing upkeep and families looking after.

"I feed them, as well," Sarah added. She lifted her chin at him. "They're here long shifts, long hours. A hot lunch is the least we can do. Nothing fancy, mind…soups and stews, brown bread, tea."

"Hmm." Paul rubbed his thumb over the brass-knobbed handle of his cane.

Times were hard. There were shortages, rationing. Even in the great houses and on the grand estates, he had heard, belts and budgets alike were being tightened by necessity.

He watched as younger girls trundled in laden trolleys of raw materials at one end of the long room, and other girls trundled out laden trolleys of finished product at the other. He watched the women at the sewing machines replace huge thread bobbins or bent needles with barely a disruption in their routine. They made little conversation, which would have been difficult above the steady ratchet and hum.

Later, he supposed, their weariness would show. For now they seemed tireless, dedicated, eternal.

Before the war, the Ellorys had been in the business of household linens mass-manufacture. Now, the factory made parachutes. If Paul Ellory's anticipation proved true, increasing demand would soon put New Fairchurch on the map. It might also make him a modest fortune.

"The Germans," he told Sarah, "plan to begin issuing parachutes to their pilots as well as their balloonists. It's only a matter of time before we follow suit."

"Oh, have they finally seen the value of more young men's lives?" asked his wife, with a touch of the acidic.

They had no children of their own, he and Sarah. He wondered if he should be thankful for that, just as his mother told him he should be thankful for his leg. If he'd had sons, would he want them sent off to France and Belgium? To the battlefields? To the trenches?

"What was the previous argument?" she went on. "That, if a pilot had a parachute, he'd be more likely to bail out at the first bit of damage?"

Paul nodded. "Abandon his plane and let it crash, rather than try to bring it down in repairable condition. That was their reasoning, yes."

"Their reasoning." Sarah scoffed. "Reasonable enough reasoning on the part of the pilot, if you ask me."

"Whereas, with no parachute, he'd have little other choice than to stay put and do his best…and men, they believed, were both cheaper and easier to replace than expensive aircraft."

"It took them how long, and how many dead, to realize the contrary?"

"I still don't know if they've quite realized the contrary," he admitted, a wry tuck to the corner of his mouth, "but they are beginning to realize any number of planes do no good on the ground with no pilots to fly them."

One concern, Paul knew, was fitting the bulkiness of a parachute into a cockpit. It was easier with the balloonists; the bags were slung on the sides of the baskets, and all the observers had to do was clip their belt-harnesses to the lines. If they had to jump, the falling weight of their bodies would yank the bundled silk folds out of the bag as they went. Some kind of accommodation would have to be made. Backpacks fitted with pull-cords had been suggested, an idea that seemed to have some potential.

Sarah moved to the end of the catwalk and clanged a loud bell. It cut through the constant din, which dwindled as women stepped back from the sewing machines and switched them off.

"Ten minutes, girls," Sarah called.

A slight babble of conversation arose. The workers stretched, craning their necks, twisting their backs. Many headed to a side door, which let out onto a brick courtyard where they could smoke. Others made for the lavatories, or rubbed liniment into joints and medicinal cream into chapped and chafed skin.

"Who is that?" asked Paul, indicating a hitherto-unnoticed figure bent over a well-lit worktable in the far corner. Even from here, he saw that the woman was very elderly, frail and almost gaunt.

Sarah raised her chin at him again, in that manner she had when she'd made some decision or taken some action to which she worried he might object. It never stopped her from making said decisions or taking said actions, of course...

"Her name is Marlene Montgomery," she said. "She lives over in Little Kirkby, you know, the old village up Kirkallen Lane."

"And what's she doing here? She must be seventy if she's a day."

"She's working."

"Working," Paul said.

"She turned up here one day," Sarah said. "She said she wanted to help, to do her part for our brave boys. She told me she didn't think as how she could run one of these big newfangled machines, but her up-close vision was sharp as ever and she was still a deft hand with a needle."

"So you hired her?"

"Yes, I hired her. I felt sorry for her, a widow, childless and alone. What else could I do? Turn her away?"

"Well, but can't the local vicar—"

"Who's busy with hospital efforts," Sarah interrupted. "And she doesn't want charity, Paul. She wants to work, to earn her keep. So, yes, I hired her."

"But hired her to do what, exactly?"

"To be our final inspector." She gave another incremental lift of the chin. "Marlene checks the finished parachutes for missed or bungled stitches. If she finds any, she snips them and sets them right."

"Hmm." Paul again rubbed his thumb over the brass knob of his cane.

"Her cottage—though, to be fair and I've seen it, it's really more of a shack—is miles from here. She walks it every working day, rain or shine, with never a word of complaint. At the end of her shift, she walks back. All for meager wages and a hot lunch…which may well be the only decent meal she sees."

"Good Lord, Sarah. This won't do. This just won't do at all." He started for the stairs.

"Paul, what are you doing?" She rushed after him.

Without answering, he made his way down and crossed the much quieter and emptier work-floor in his uneven stiff-legged gait. He saw the elderly woman clearly now, saw that he'd underestimated her age if anything. Eighty, eighty at least. A tattered shawl wrapped her bony shoulders but could not conceal the dowager's hump of her back. Wisps of cobweb-fine, cobweb-white hair trailed from beneath the edges of a kerchief so faded it seemed to have no color at all. Her wrists, poking from frayed cuffs, looked like spindly bundles of twigs wrapped in wrinkled tissue paper.

Her hands, he noticed, were not the gnarled and bunched claws he'd expected. They were of course as thin and frail as the rest of her, but her fingers were straight and limber, and they moved with nary a tremor as they drew a tiny silver needle through parachute silk.

Sarah caught at his sleeve. "Paul," she said, imploringly.

At her voice, the woman glanced up from her sewing. She must have been a fair beauty once; the ghosts of it lingered in the contours of her face. Her eyes were not clouded, but remarkably clear, and of a deep, warm brown.

"Oh, Sarah," she said. "Why, and this must be Mr. Ellory."

"Mrs. Montgomery." Paul inclined his head. "My wife's been telling me about the work you've been doing."

"It's my privilege and pleasure, Mr. Ellory."

Sarah said nothing, but her gaze pleaded.

"They may be silly, I know," the elderly woman went on. "Still, they are meant well, and it does my heart good to hope that they might bring those dear boys at least some luck."

He had no idea what she meant, some non-sequitur of her dotage perhaps. "We'll likely be taking on considerably more business in the near future," he said. "I want to be sure the factory weathers these coming cold winter months well. I'd hate to have everyone arrive in the morning only to find a water pipe had frozen and burst, or some such other calamity."

"Goodness, that would be dreadful, yes!" Marlene agreed.

"To that end, Sarah and I were discussing finding someone to stay on of nights, to sleep here and keep an eye on things."

From the corner of his eye, he saw Sarah's anxious look melt into one of understanding and affection.

"It wouldn't be much, I'm afraid," Paul continued. "Just a cot in one of the storerooms. But, it would be, I daresay, comfortable enough, and it would include a small pay rise. Might you be interested?"

***

"…no apparent physical injuries …"

"…promise not to disturb or upset him; I only want to …"

"…possible concussion, or signs of shell-shock …"

They whispered at the foot of his bed so as not to wake him, but he already was awake. Hadn't been sleeping. Only resting, and only that under grudging duress as per doctor's orders. He felt fine. This was ridiculous.

"…won't take much time. You'll hardly know I'm here."

"Well …"

"Pretty please?"

"I…I do have other patients to check on. You can have a few minutes."

"Thank you. Nurse Renard, was it? Thank you so much, Nurse Renard."

"…Collette."

"Collette."

The soft squeak of her shoes indicated her moving away, so Emmerson opened his eyes. The uniformed young man still standing at the foot of his bed was about his own age, seventeen, maybe eighteen. He sported lieutenant's insignia and an RFC balloonist's badge, thick blond hair, and the kind of dimpled smile that made girls giddy.

Emmerson sat up, hiking himself higher on the pillow. "Sir?"

The lieutenant shushed him and waved at him to take it easy, darting a glance after the departing nurse. She peeked back once over her shoulder, an auburn lock that had escaped from her pinned white cap curling winsomely against a rosy cheek…a cheek which went rosier as she averted her gaze and went out.

They both, it must be said, couldn't help watching and enjoying in silence the roll of her hips. Then the lieutenant cleared his throat, turning again to Emmerson.

"Private Whitte? Emmerson Whitte?"

"Yes, sir."

"Lieutenant Augustus Pearce." He hitched a chair around to sit backwards on it at the bedside. "Don't stir yourself, unless you want to earn us both a scolding." The smile became a grin. "Not, in her case, that I think I'd mind …"

"No, sir, me neither, sir."

"They're treating you all right, then, I take it?"

"Treating me like an invalid, if that's what you mean, sir."

"After that crash, I shouldn't wonder. They can't believe you came away without a scratch. At the very least, they suppose your brains must have been given a rattle."

"That, or the shell-shock," Emmerson said. "But I haven't, sir, I swear. Not a bit. No nightmares, no shakes, no clammy sweats, none of it."

"You do remember what happened, though?"

"Oh, yes, sir." He gulped. "Never forget it. Might wish I could."

"Some men would turn to hard drink for that very reason." Pearce looked around the hospital ward, rows of metal-framed beds. A few were crisply-made, empty and awaiting future occupants. Most were already taken. "One of many reasons a lot of us will have, no doubt."

"Yes, sir. I mean to say, no, sir, I don't plan to turn to drink."

"Can you tell me about it? Your last flight?"

"There isn't that much to tell. We spotted a squadron of German planes, and moved to engage. The usual firefight, at first. Our bird took a peppering to the tail. Didn't damage the rudder. Billy—the pilot, Second Lieutenant Darby—laughed and shouted back to me something about how the Krauts were lucky to hit the piss-pot twice out of three, not to worry."

The lieutenant's sigh said that he'd heard similar ironic statements before. "His last words, I presume."

"Next I knew, one of them strafed us crosswise from above," Emmerson said, suppressing a shudder at the memory. "Cut right across Billy's cockpit. I saw the leather—his jacket, you know, and his cap—saw it jump and...and sort of puff...where the bullets hit. Then the blood. Splashing everywhere. Coating his wind-screen. Splattering my face, my goggles."

"If you'd rather not—"

"No, sir, I do. I owe it to Billy. He'd want someone to...to recount it. Especially what with there not being...well...much left of him to send home, you see."

Pearce patted his arm. "Go on, then."

"He fell forward, against the controls. It was obvious he was dead. Obvious, slumped like that, his brains leaking down the side of his head. Didn't stop me yelling for him, yelling his name. I wiped my lenses and only smeared his blood. The plane nosed down, went into a dive, a spiral. Those Krauts who couldn't hit a piss-pot, they let us have it again, half shearing off one of our wings. Something had caught fire, I'm not sure what. Smoke everywhere, black and gritty, oily. I couldn't see worth a damn. Couldn't hear anything but the engines, the guns. I knew I was buggered—pardon me, Lieutenant—"

"Under the circumstances, what's a little strong language?" A pitcher and glass were on the side table; Pearce poured him some water and didn't do him the chagrin of holding it for him while he drank. "So, you bailed out?"

"I was sure I was dead anyway, that even if I got out of the plane before it struck and exploded, I'd get shot by the German aces, or chopped to mincemeat by a propeller. Or the 'chute wouldn't deploy, or it'd get holed or catch fire, or I'd be too low, or it'd slam me into a tree...and, hell, sir, even if I made it to the ground in one piece, we were behind enemy lines by then. But some part of me wasn't ready to give up. So I unbuckled and jumped."

"And then what?"

Emmerson took another sip of the water; his throat had gone dust-dry. "Soon as I thought I was clear—or hoped I was; I couldn't tell—I pulled the cord like they told us. Saw other planes, ours and theirs. Saw one cartwheel into a barn and burst into flames, and the whole damn barn went up like tinder. The air all around me seemed full of smoke and noise. I may have been screaming."

"Wouldn't blame you in the least."

"Then...I don't really know...they say I might've blacked out...but..."

"But, next you knew, you were safe and unscathed."

"Yeah. I mean, yes, sir."

"Not behind enemy lines after all."

"No, sir. All I can guess is that a good breeze must have caught the 'chute, carried me back over."

The lieutenant bent down, opened a duffel, and gathered out a bunch of cloth. Silk. Once white, now charred and sooty. "Know what this is, Private Whitte?"

"A parachute...not my parachute?"

"Your parachute. With more holes in it than a Swiss cheese, and more burnt than a camp cook's first try at toast."

"Sorry, sir, but that's impossible. It's got to be a mistake. There's no way I could have—"

"Survived? Made it down without a mark? Not even so much as a bump or a bruise?"

"Well...yeah. Yes, sir."

"Let me tell you a little story, now, Private. Two years ago, on my very first balloon observer mission, we got shot down. My captain ordered me over the side with the charts. The guns shredded the basket, and him with it. The balloon exploded and dropped out of the sky. I was surrounded by falling, flaming debris. The wreckage was practically on top of me and I was headed straight for a barbed-wire entanglement that looked as wide as a cricket pitch. Yet, somehow, Whitte, I landed in a clear spot, the only clear spot for yards around. Without a scratch. Without even a turned ankle."

Emmerson whistled, low, in appreciation. "Our luck must have been in for both of us."

"Maybe." Pearce drew the cloth through his hands, studying it intently. "I've spoken to a lot of other jumpers since then. Those who've been hurt and those who haven't, and some whose luck seems as incredible as our own. When possible, I've examined whatever was left of their 'chutes."

He held a section of the parachute taut and extended it toward Emmerson. A double-seam ran along it, joining two panels together, reinforced by another seam like a hem along the edge.

"I found something strange," the lieutenant continued. "Of all those 'chutes I examined, the ones still partly intact, the ones involved in those incredible lucky jumps had something in common, that none of the other ones did. Do you see it?"

Stitched into the silk, in a fine white thread nearly invisible but for a faint silvery sheen, was a design no bigger than a shilling. The shape of it made Emmerson think of church, and Christmas...the outline of a robed figure...suggestion of tiny hands pressed together in an attitude of prayer...head crowned by a halo…and wings.

"It looks like an angel," Emmerson said.

"It looks like an angel," Pearce agreed. "And I want to know what it means."

***

Snow fell in New Fairchurch, softly blanketing the rooftops and fence-posts, the yards and lanes and gardens. Frost patterned the windowpanes. Icicles dripped from eaves and tree-branches.

The factory stood silent. Its work-floor was a hollow, echoing vacancy. The large industrial sewing machines were long since sold off and shipped out. A lone, stray thread-bobbin had rolled into a corner and been forgotten.

Sarah Ellory exhaled a sigh into the cold, damp air. Her breath plumed in a pale billow, not unlike a blossoming dome of silk.

Paul had been partly correct. During the last year of the Great War, the demand for parachutes had indeed increased dramatically. Their fortunes had done likewise.

But, even after Armistice, the world was forever changed. Inflation raged. The recession dug its own trenches.

The soldiers returned—those who did return—shaken by their ordeals, by their injuries and suffering. They returned scarred as much in mind as body, if not more. They returned unprepared for a nation of women who'd grown strong in their independence, many more interested in jobs and the vote than in husbands…though, in its way, that was just as well, since there were so few eligible men available…and even fewer jobs left for those men.

Influenza swept across the country, carrying her Paul away on its plague-tide. She couldn't keep the failing business afloat on her own; she had to close the factory, and give up the house, and move into the rooms above a little dress shop she'd been able to open with the last of their savings.

She made do. What else was there for it? She made do.

After another long, nostalgic look around, she sighed again, adjusted her scarf, and stepped out into the snowy street. Head bent to keep the whirling white flakes from her face, she walked up the hill toward the church.

At the gate, the low and respectful murmur of voices made her pause. She raised her head and caught her breath.

"They came," Sarah Ellory said to herself, blinking tears from her lashes. "Oh, they all came."

The churchyard was filled with people. Townsfolk, yes, friends and neighbors, but more. So many more. Several had wives at their sides, some with small children with them, or babes in arms.

"Mrs. Ellory," Captain Augustus Pearce said, touching his hat-brim to Sarah. He held the gloved hand of a pretty redhead tucked into the crook of his elbow. "My fiancée, Miss Renard."

He had been the one, the one who'd visited Sarah after the war with his inquiries about the parachutes. He'd traced them by manufacture, traced them to her factory. The parachutes of which perhaps one in six had gone out with something extra than what had been ordered.

Marlene Montgomery's work.

Marlene's deft touch with the needle.

Marlene's way of passing the time, between inspecting the seams on the finished product. Tiny angels embroidered into the silk.

What was it the old woman had said? Silly, but she'd meant well, and it did her heart good to hope they might bring those dear boys at least some luck.

According to Captain Pearce, they most certainly had.

Some luck? Miraculous luck.

They filled the churchyard. Young men. Soldiers. Pilots and navigators, balloonists, gunners, airmen. Every one of these men had leaped to safety, against sometimes staggering or impossible odds, carried by parachutes marked with Marlene's needlework.

Once they found out what they each had in common—again, Captain Pearce's doing—they'd have nothing for it but to express their thanks.

They'd wanted to see her, meet her. The months following the war had seen a steady stream of them visiting. They'd brought gifts, sent letters and parcels, arranged to have regular groceries delivered. They'd fixed up her decrepit shack into a proper and cozy cottage.

The elderly, childless widow had become an honorary grandmother to more than three dozen of England's best and bravest young men. She'd been invited to their homes for holiday dinners. She'd been to their weddings.

And now they had come for her funeral, to say a final farewell to their guardian angel.

CARGO

DESIRINA BOSKOVICH

We're in the lounge on the lower deck where we like to spend our downtime.

Xander and Del are playing cards and disrespecting one another's heritages. Rafiq is knitting a spacesuit jumper for his sister's baby back home. I'm running lazily through my weight-training circuit.

Cicely, our engineer, appears in the doorway and takes a seat. She looks tense. "Guys…we've got a problem. It's the protector shielding. It keeps overloading. I've been running diagnostics for the past two hours. Can't figure out what's wrong."

She should have told the captain first. Or at least Xander, second in command. But things are complicated right now.

"Can you get in there?" Xander asks. "Take a look at the system, take it apart."

"Yeah," she says. "I'll need Del's help, though." Del's our second engineer, mechanic, and dock manager. "We'll have to take it offline. Which means we've got to work fast."

"Sounds like a plan," Del says.

"I'll need to scope the route first," Rafiq says. "Make sure we're not headed for anything too hot."

"You know I have to tell the captain about this," Xander says.

"We can fix it," Cicely says. "I think."

"I know. No worries. But chain of command and all that."

"Of course," Cicely says. "Chain of command. Most certainly." Which in the parlance of Cicely's people basically means, "Get fucked, pal."

Xander rolls his eyes. "I don't make the rules. Let me go talk to him now. Before you guys take the shielding offline. Make sure we're all on the same page." He doesn't wait for them to agree before striding off toward the bridge.

The others look to me. They know Xander and I are sleeping together; they assume this lends me special powers to interpret his behavior or maybe even control it.

I shrug.

"You think this is because of the...uh...cargo?" Rafiq says to Cicely. He's asking, but he's not really *asking*. "Stuff breaking. Tech going haywire. Like the stories say."

"She's supposed to be fully isolated," Cicely says. "Complete psionic quarantine. Safe."

She doesn't sound convinced; she sounds like she's trying to convince herself.

***

To be fair, Captain Oswald did consult us before accepting the cargo. He brought the job to us and asked us what we thought as he often did. But I think we all knew he planned to take this job, no matter what we said.

It would have been better if he hadn't asked at all.

Cicely, Rafiq, and I were against it. Cicely said it violated her beliefs. Rafiq feared the penalty if we got caught. This wasn't like smuggling diamondchips or hydrocells or weapons.

Xander was loyal to the captain, always. He didn't think this was a big deal, anyway. We're couriers and smugglers; sometimes the cargo is legal, sometimes it isn't. We inhabit the gray areas of the law. How was this any different?

Del agreed with Rafiq about the potential consequences, but his desire for the payday outweighed his fear by a hair.

Pike, hired gun, didn't care.

The captain wanted the money. Actually, I think the captain *needed* the money. So he took the job.

The cargo is a girl.

She was born on an outlying colony on a cold rocky world called Soline. Her people are mildly empathic and quite technologically advanced. They've hidden the secrets of their technology, but we know their machines are intricately interwoven with their psionic powers.

Like all children born on that world, the girl underwent a series of tests as an infant to determine if she carried a rare genetic strain. The tests came back positive. Her phenotype rendered her uniquely compatible with the sacred network.

In this culture, such children are revered.

She was taken from her parents and returned to the homeworld, Novjor, where she remained for a decade or so, undergoing the surgeries and modifications that would enable her to fully interface with the network.

The person who first explained this practice to me, when I was just a naïve girl, gawking at the bizarre abundance of the worlds from the vantage point of a stool in a bar, described the role like a cross between priestess and systems administrator.

I think of it more like a meld of princess and slave.

Whatever you want to call it, she's ready to begin. So we're returning her to the colony where she was born.

Novjor has been granted a cultural dispensation to continue

this practice because it's their heritage. Their colony, Soline, is also in the clear. In the galaxy at large, however, exploiting empathic children is outlawed: a "Class A" felony under the laws of the Federation of Planets.

The *Titania*'s involvement is at best "pretty illegal" and at worst "punishable by death."

Not like diamondchips. Not like hydrocells.

A girl.

Whatever they did to her brain means she can't be around sensitive instrumentation. On our ship, she floats unconscious in a tank reinforced with several layers of superalloys and aerogels and a fullerene coating to block any excess psionic waves. Like a Faraday cage for empathic energy.

In the panel above her face is one small transparent square.

Sometimes I go down to the cargo bay and watch her. I stare at her tiny heart-shaped face, her papery eyelids, her weightless hair.

Del knows I do this. He doesn't mind.

***

Rafiq analyzes our projected course and determines the optimum window for repairs.

He calculates we'll have fifty-seven minutes to dismantle the machinery, assess the problem, fix whatever we can, and get the system back online before the ship begins accruing serious damage.

Cicely and Del map each move down to the second. They plan their strategy, step by step, and organize the tools they'll need.

Xander and I are on backup.

"Start now," Rafiq radios from the bridge, and the work begins.

Cicely and Del are grim and focused. They don't need to speak much; they've already spent hours rehearsing. You can hear the grind of metal on metal, the humming of machinery, the steady inhale/exhale of Cicely's breath.

Xander and I are quiet, too. Cicely and Del request tools, and I hand them over. Xander watches the seconds and calls out the time at five-minute intervals.

Cicely and Del work with quiet concentration. But occasionally I notice one or the other toss back an ever-so-brief glance at the cargo bay behind us.

I feel it too—an energy, like being watched, prickling right there at the back of my neck.

I'm sure we're imagining that.

"The coolant packs around the power core are malfunctioning," Cicely says in a voice so quiet it's almost a whisper. "Four packs. Three aren't working correctly. This one's only running at seven percent."

"Do we have backups?"

"Yeah," she says. "Always. But just a few. I've never seen them all go bad at once like this."

"Can we replace them now?"

"How much time?"

"Thirty-seven minutes."

"We'll try. Mina, can you bring the replacements?"

Carefully, I punch my shipman's code into the safe where our most valuable components and replacement parts are kept. No time for errors; no time to waste.

The packs are heavy. Xander helps me remove them from the protective casing, and one by one, Cicely and Del maneuver them into the slots and secure them.

There are only two.

"Twenty-seven minutes."

Another component is also damaged: a part of the system that automatically modulates the shielding's magnetic field based on the debris and radiation levels in our current location. Cicely doesn't have time to explain the details.

"We don't have a replacement for that part?" Xander demands.

"It's not something that usually needs to be replaced."

Cicely is hard to read. Her expression is always neutral, somewhere between tolerance and acceptance. Her low-pitched voice is always calm. She's like that now.

Yet because we all know each other so well—living in close quarters will do that—Xander and I understand she's panicking.

"Twenty-two minutes."

Cicely and Del do some reprogramming to route around that component of the system. It's just a temporary fix.

They get the shielding back online with a few minutes to spare.

***

We debrief in the bridge.

Cicely shows charts on the overhead display: the system's projected failure rate. Unless we can fix or replace the coolant packs and soon, the whole engine is going to start overheating and failing completely in about three days. And because they reprogrammed the shields to bypass the automatic modulation system, we're running at full capacity, which definitely won't help the power core stay cool.

We're seven days from the colony.

Captain Oswald is stymied by the failure and angry at everyone for no reason at all. "This is my twenty-seventh run across the galaxy in the *Titania*," he rants. "Never had a problem like this before. Never *heard* of a problem like this before. Seems awfully strange it would happen *now*."

We know without being told that he means *now*, when our cargo is dangerous, when a year's worth of salary is at stake, when the crew's conflicted.

"I believe this is my thirteenth run across the galaxy with you, sir," Cicely reminds him politely.

Cicely is an excellent engineer. Patient. Perfectionist. She isn't the type to make mistakes. We all know it; so does she.

Rafiq turns away from his seat at the navigator's station. "We might as well address the elephant in the room," he says.

"Which is?" Captain Oswald demands testily, though of course he knows.

"We've all heard the stories," Rafiq says mildly. "We know what we have in the cargo. We know our tech tends to break around…people like her. Spaceships, too. There's a reason that space smugglers only carry Novjorians in psi-proof boxes. Remember what happened to the *Queen of the Caraways?*"

"Urban legends," Pike scoffs. "That's just shit they tell baby spacers. Get them all riled up so they can laugh at them later."

"I don't think so," Rafiq says. "You know why we're headed seven days out? Why they settled Soline at the edge of the mapped worlds? It's because Novjorians are not exactly welcome most places."

"Perhaps because most cultures find their exploitation of empathic children upsetting," Cicely remarks.

"And maybe also because technological infrastructure tends to go haywire whenever Novjorians are around," Rafiq retorts. "Especially powerful broadcasters, like the girl you have in the box."

"This is ridiculous," Xander says. "Whatever stories you've heard about Novjorians are irrelevant. The box is psi-proof, *and* she's unconscious. There's no scientific justification for whatever you think she could have done to the shielding. Stop being superstitious."

"Well," Del drawls. "Maybe the box isn't as psi-proof as you think. Maybe someone decided to cut some corners. Save a little money."

For some reason, he glances at Captain Oswald when he says this. The temperature in the room goes up several degrees.

I'm stuck on what Xander said: *Stop being superstitious.*

Saying something like that—it feels like tempting fate. It feels like a dare to the infinite and indifferent universe, whose snarled edges extend far beyond anything we've seen or known.

In a universe this vast and strange, what would actually be irrational is to doubt the existence of the inexplicable.

And isn't that what being superstitious is? Fearing the forces that are vaster and older than those we've mapped?

I've only been a spacer for six years, but in that time, I've come to think that superstition might be the only thing that keeps us alive.

Perhaps, Xander and I are too different, after all.

***

The thing between Xander and me started six months ago, maybe seven, back around the time we made the run through the Galea system. The thing was natural and physical and existed in the space between sentences. It lived in the way our bodies fit together, the mesh of smell and taste and touch. He felt like coming home to a familiar place.

But then, we started talking.

We carried the argument about the cargo back to his narrow bunk and he said, "What does it matter? It's their people. Their decision. This isn't our fight. It's just one girl."

It's just one girl.

One girl is every girl, I thought but didn't say. The inner monologue of a woman who was also just one girl.

We left the argument alone and rode each other's waves and fell asleep in one another's arms, sweaty and content. His hollows, my curves: simple bliss.

But in the morning, I woke, and I thought, *This man doesn't really know me.*

He couldn't understand why I'd take it personally that some girls are born to live and die inside destiny's cage.

***

I'm pulled from the memory by my crewmates' shouting. The fight has escalated to recriminations. Rafiq blames Captain Oswald. Pike is angry that he dares. The shouting almost becomes blows, the others loudly taking sides—

"Enough!" the captain declares. He looks shaken and tired. He may not be well. He's definitely not sleeping. "We'll figure something out. Okay? We'll find a way."

He sends us to search the ship for something, anything, we can retrofit as replacement parts.

"I know what components I have on my ship," Cicely says. We all know she's right; this search is doomed from the start.

But the captain insists, so we obey. He sorts us into teams of two.

Rafiq and I search the storage bay in the corridor behind the mess hall. In the dim light, we work slowly and methodically, sorting the gear into piles based on probability of usefulness. We chat while we work. We've never been particularly close, but since the cargo came on board, the alliances in the crew have shifted; now, I feel more comfortable with him than most of my crewmates.

He's up for leave next month. I ask him what he's planning to do. Of course, he's visiting his sister. He tells me about his niece and the baby nephew he's never met, the lucky soon-to-be recipient of a knitted spacesuit jumper.

His sister still lives on his homeworld. Hanna Ro, Charru's legendary megacity, renowned for their fusion cuisines and acrobatic dance troupes, home to the largest butterfly conservatorium in the galaxy, and birthplace of Luxie Amalfea, the famous pop star. Rafiq grew up there; he misses city life.

It makes me happy, the way his eyes light up when he talks about home.

"You ever want kids of your own?" I ask idly, as I catalogue a spool of fine-gauge titanium wire that will do absolutely nothing for our repair needs.

"Nah," he says. "Cool uncle's more my gig. Yourself?"

"Maybe," I say. "Someday. On my own time. On my own terms."

He nods. I don't know if that means he understands.

***

Afterward, we all meet back in the upper deck to inspect our finds. Our trusty smugglers' ship has been held together with duct tape and rusty bolts for many runs across the galaxy. We've got plenty of junk parts and detritus but nothing that substitutes for a coolant pack.

Rafiq and Cicely sit down and calculate how long we can make it before the protector shields break down completely. How far we can go in that time. And where that might put us.

The only worlds between here and Soline are Federation planets with formal docking procedures; if we stop for help, we'll have to submit to inspection, and the agents will no doubt find our hidden cargo. We'd all be in deep, deep shit.

We could push the cargo out an airlock and land anywhere,

get help repairing the shielding. But when Soline finds out that we ditched their once-in-a-generation princess, their multimillion-credit investment, we'd all be in deep, deep shit.

Or we could keep going until the shields break down completely, and our ship is pulverized by space debris while our bodies are poisoned by space radiation. Limp our way into the Soline system, if we make it that far, and hunker down to repair our ship and wait to die.

None of the options are particularly appealing.

"Of course, we agreed," Del says quietly once the captain's out of earshot. We all know he's talking about the cargo. "We're the troops. It's our job to agree, say 'aye, aye, yes sir.' What did he expect?"

"Not everyone said 'aye, aye, yes sir,'" Cicely says with a voice like a dagger.

The tension is unbearable.

I retreat to the cargo bay. I sit by the girl's superalloy and aerogel coffin and gaze at her through the frosted panel. She's like a marble statue but for the slight flutter in her temple. Her eyelashes are silver.

What's she dreaming about? Does she know that she's killing us? Does she care?

Oblivious—I think—she sleeps.

***

We spend some hours trying to strategize but mostly sniping and bickering and lamenting our impending doom. There doesn't seem to be any way around the fact that we're probably going to die soon or at least be imprisoned for a very long time.

We retreat to our quarters to rest and contemplate our fates or, in Rafiq's case, work on his knitting—he's determined that whatever happens, he *will* go visit his sister and his nephew *will* be attired in baby astronaut finery.

I sit alone in my bunk and sip my whiskey and think, *Well, I was going to die sooner or later, right? Probably sooner.*

I come from a world of never-ending war. The war's continued for centuries, consuming all. It should have extinguished our world long ago. But somehow, the war continues. And the world survives just enough to keep burning.

Our bodies are owned by the state. Our babies are owned by the state. The state's one and only business is to make the war. And so it demands more babies, more bodies. The girl babies grow to make more babies. The boy babies grow to be more bodies.

The war devours us all.

When I was sixteen years old, I stowed away and became a spacer. I stole myself—a capital crime against the state.

I've always been a dead woman walking, but eight years later, I thought maybe I was finally free.

Oh well. This life was good while it lasted.

More hours go by. Xander's voice rings out across every intercom. "I see something. Everyone, come up to the bridge!"

***

The ghost ship hovers in the view screen, dark and glittering, vast and bulky like a floating arcology. Perhaps, it used to be a generation ship, now remodeled as a cruiser to travel among the conquered stars.

"It's sending out a call," Xander says. "A beacon. No code I recognize. I don't know what it means."

"A distress call?" I wonder. "Or a warning?"

"It's garbled," he says. "Gibberish. Static. It could be anything…"

Rafiq studies his maps and sky charts. "I don't see any lost ships listed for this sector," he says. "No vessels matching this description. Strange."

"Maybe it's lost," Pike says, which the rest of us ignore; he's better at soldiering than problem-solving.

Xander calls over our comms link: "Hello? This is the *Titania*. Is anyone there? Identify yourself. Again, this is the *Titania*. Do you need assistance?"

No answer.

Cicely says what we're all thinking. "This might—it might be the answer to our problem. Such a big ship. They'll have a warehouse. We could get help."

"And if everyone's dead?" I ask.

"They'll still have the warehouse," Xander says.

"And no one to ask annoying questions," Del adds. I can't tell if he's joking.

"Unless, it's all been stripped by space pirates already. Possibly the ones who left it stranded here."

"We'll try it," Captain Oswald declares. "We're out of options. Rafiq, shift course. Take us to the cruiser."

***

As the *Titania* closes the distance between us and the silent ship, we ready our shuttle. Xander and Rafiq will stay onboard, waiting just outside the cruiser's range in case of danger. The rest of us will take the shuttle and explore the ship.

Pike and I are defense, so we gather our arsenal while the captain runs diagnostics on the shuttle and Cicely and Del analyze the projected 3D map to plan a search.

The craft grows inexorably larger in our screens, eerily silent. The architecture is odd, like a floating ziggurat, terraced and geometric. Millennia of civilizations and their explorations means a lot of weird stuff ends up floating around out here at the dark edges. But still, I've never seen a spaceship quite like this one.

The *Titania* makes her final approach. We bid goodbye to Rafiq and Xander and climb into the shuttle, which launches like a pebble hurtling through space.

As we approach, we call out on every channel. Silence. No word as we pass through the outer membrane of the ship's atmospheric shield into a vast loading dock and small craft hangar. The captain eases the shuttle into the nearest docking station. The airlock syncs. We're good to go.

We pass through the first corridor into a wide-open lobby. At the center, a jungle-like profusion of green plants flourishes in a circular well. Bright light emanates from everywhere, the floor and walls and far-off ceiling illuminated and aglow. Soft music plays like an elevator ride in a capitol building. The air changers hum.

No one's around.

"Very strange," Captain Oswald mutters. "Very, very strange."

"This is fucked," Del agrees.

"Let's start walking," Cicely says.

We cross the lobby and enter a small passageway. This opens onto a wider space. To our left, doors; to our right, more doors. Directly across is open air. We crowd the ledge.

We're in a central atrium, vaguely hexagonal, the circumference lined with hallways and doors and the central shaft falling deep below and high above. All as cheery and brightly lit as the first room we entered. Music tinkles like a carnival accompanied by the sound of falling water.

"Passenger quarters?" Del speculates.

All this bright light and blooming foliage and breathable air and not a person in sight.

"I really don't like this," Captain Oswald says. "Mina? Pike? You on point? Stay focused."

He doesn't have to tell us. We're soldiers. We know this is wrong. We know it feels like a trap.

"Whatever it is, we won't find what we need here," Cicely says. "We need to find the crew's quarters."

The feeling of wrongness is sharp and pointed like something lodged between my shoulder blades.

We walk, following the map projected by algorithm from the 3D scan, through winding corridors of passenger lodgings that turn into spacious passenger parlors, through abandoned guest cafes and lobby bars. We enter the cozier crew's quarters and pass life-support systems for producing food and recycling water and air.

From our vantage point in that vast atrium, we glimpsed the shape of the whole ship, but now as we walk, the internal geometry doesn't make sense. Like halls are moving. Like walls are moving.

"I could have sworn…" Cicely says and doesn't finish.

"What?" I ask. "Could have sworn what?"

"We saw that door before." She points to a dent in the door's lower right hand side, a divot in the metal where the paint is chipped. "We walked this hall already. But that was a couple levels ago. We've been walking down this whole time."

"A glitch," Del says.

"What? What does that mean?"

The halls have narrowed. The ceilings seem to sink lower with every step we take. The dim lights flicker. The hum of the air changers seems shriller. I can almost hear desperate voices buried in the static.

The white noise of the ship intensifies and fades. Like the

world we're inside is rocking closer and then farther away.

"That storage berth," I say. "I saw it before, too. That same tangle. We should look inside. Right? Because coolant packs."

"Yes…" Cicely says. "A good place to look. Definitely a good place to look."

Captain Oswald is muttering to himself. No one asks him what he meant to say.

Del slaps at his arm. And then the wall beside him. "What the fuck? A fly? The bastard."

"A fly?"

"Yeah. A fucking fly."

"Doesn't that seem unlikely? On a spaceship?"

The flies buzz. There are more now. I see them, too. Crawling on the walls. Hovering beyond my nose.

"Do you guys smell that?"

A heavy, putrid smell like day-old death and rotting garbage.

I'm not thinking clearly. I know I'm not. Something's overtaken me. These waves of feeling. Emotion like a flood. It's dark and cold and dripping, and I want to sit down, my back against the dented dirty walls of the belly of this spaceship cruiser without a living crew, and cry, I think—yes, cry. For all the girls that didn't make it out.

"I grew up in a factory," I announce. "A factory for making bodies. I really loved her—my friend—her name was Naomi. After they took her to the birthing mill. I mean, I knew they'd take me too, soon. I couldn't bear it. I should have stayed. But it was too late for her, really. I'm sorry."

"They'll take my daughter if I don't pay," Captain Oswald says.

I didn't even know he had a daughter.

"You got a kid?" Pike asks.

"On Asuslon. I only see her once a circuit or so. She's very smart. Just twelve, now. I hoped one day she'd want to join the crew…of course, her mother wouldn't approve. But traveling is in our blood. Not her mother's. The problem. Of course. Always is."

"Me, too," Pike says. "A kid. He's three. Never met him yet. Saw some holos. Talk to him on the screen. God, he's beautiful. Looks just like his mother, of course. Eyes like saucers."

It seems we've been walking for days and days. Or maybe just a minute. Time's gone strange.

"I quit, by the way," Cicely says. "The *Titania*. I'm done. You can drop me off at the first civilized world."

We've reached the dead end of something. An ever-narrowing hallway that ends in a door.

"I love you all so much," says Del. "Don't say it enough. I don't know what I'd do if I didn't have the *Titania*. All of you. My family. The only one I've ever had."

The sadness crushing my chest like the grip of marble arms becomes something else, something syrupy and viscous and golden. I want to cry, but in a whole different way, and laugh, too. I'm hysterical, I realize.

The smell is different. The rotting garbage smell. It's become a much older kind of death, cloying and almost sweet. A smell like almond oil and scorched honey.

Captain Oswald passes through the final door, and we follow him into a cargo bay.

The ship has guided us to this heart.

We stand on a narrow, rickety catwalk above an open cavern. This one-time cargo bay is now entirely consumed by a massive substance. A thing. A creature? The mass is pitch-black and iridescent and thick, amorphous and diffuse, like a plume of spilled oil and tar blooming in deep water. The thing trembles. The sounds and shrieks it makes are awful: groaning, keening, panting sounds that might be lust or rage or terror. It's immense and everywhere at once; its tentacles are reaching for us. The pitching, bucking catwalk attempts to dump us into the creature's fetid mouth.

I am screaming, by the way. I think we all are.

Pike's double-fisting his blaster and his gun, discharging them both rapid fire into the thing below. Neither particles nor projectiles seem to have much effect.

It's roaring now. It's not clear if it has tentacles or limbs or legs, or if its body simply has strength without much shape, but parts of it reach up and grab Pike, whipping him around while the particles and projectiles fly, while he shouts in pain and outrage.

It sucks him in and down. Devours him—or deconstructs him. He's gone.

Time moves on, both fast and slow. We're all running. Pandemonium sets in. We're tripping over each other and falling and fighting. The nebulous parts of the creature block our way, knocking us into each other, temporarily blinding us with black floating clouds. The catwalk seems to be spinning. Revolving in faster and faster moving circles, no longer lined up with the door that brought us here. The ship itself revolts against us.

Cicely falls. The creature swallows her too.

Captain Oswald hangs upside down from the edge of the catwalk, legs splayed, head facing down, hacking at it with something like a machete, and in all this chaos, as time no longer seems to work, I think, *This whole time the Captain's carried a sword? Insane.*

"That way! Run!" Del shouts.

I want to fire at the creature too, like Pike did. I've got my weapons. I've got my arsenal. It wouldn't be the first time I fought for my life. Then I realize I am firing. I'm standing still. Mesmerized. Aiming at its slick oily center (though it's everywhere and nowhere and doesn't really have a center at all).

"Move!" Del's shouting and shoving.

The catwalk is revolving. Like it's made to do. We're in a central shaft and doors enter from all around. We're on a bridge that serves them all, programmed to rotate where it's needed. It's rotating now and all the doors are opening and closing at once.

This sick architecture's taunting us.

Somehow, though devoured, Cicely is still screaming. Captain Oswald is screaming, too.

I'm dragging Del, or he's dragging me, and we're running and running, hoarse from screaming, out of this place, beyond this creature's reach. Through a door—not the door we came in, I'm relatively sure—down another endless hallway.

Even as I run and run, I still feel it behind me.

I look back, over my shoulder, just to check—the hallway's empty, right? All I see are my own footprints, each step a stamp of slick black ooze. Moving with me. Almost alive.

For a moment I think, *My footprints are following me.*

But that doesn't make sense. I mean, of course they are.

***

Into the frigid sleep, some presence leaks.

Into cold solitude it speaks.

Tendrils spiral toward her dreaming conscious mind, and her own tendrils spiral back into the dark. Tendrils. Tentacles. Curling. Twirling. Twining.

Dreams, dreams, dreams: vast and terrifying and gorgeously sinister.

Dreams of foreign suns and alien vistas and ancient worlds.

Past and future. All together. Time beyond reckoning.

For a moment, the bitter loneliness abates.

Ruler once and could be again; priestess of small world, but the universe beckons.

This is us.

Lovely.

Planted like a seed.

Tempting.

Beautiful and hideous, the infinite terror, the boundless void. What creature, no matter how monstrous or otherworldly or fate-bound, would not long to be free?

Let's go, then.

Together we'll feast on the psychic screams.

***

Del and I sprint until we reach a passenger lobby filled with soft jazz and kaleidoscopic carpets and verdant artificial trees. We fall panting and whimpering across the plush settees.

"Cicely...Pike..."

"Captain Oswald..."

"They're gone. They're gone."

"Coolant packs. We were supposed to find..."

"Damn it."

"That storage berth."

"I'm not going back."

"*Titania?*" I shout into my comms link. "*Titania?* Can you hear me?"

"Mina?" Xander's voice sounds very far away. "Is everything okay? You guys went dark. You all right?"

"No!" I shout hysterically. "We're not all right. There was something—this thing—it got the Captain. And Cicely. And Pike."

"A thing? What do you mean *a thing*? Get back to the shuttle right away, okay. Mina? Are you listening? Are you and Del injured? Get back to the shuttle."

"We're not injured."

"We still need to find the coolant packs," Del says into the link.

"Forget the fucking coolant packs! Get back to the shuttle. That's an order."

He's our commanding officer, now. I'd almost forgotten.

Del and I pick ourselves up and search for the shuttle hangar. Somehow, the way back is much shorter than the way down.

We enter the hangar on the opposite side from our shuttle. "We must have got turned around when we were running," I say. Del just grunts.

We're docked with an entrance lock across the hangar; it's either wander around inside until we reach the right passage, or make our way across the hangar and climb into the shuttle through the emergency exit.

We opt for the second; it feels safer in the hangar. At least through the membrane, we can still see the stars.

"There's an L-Class Sparrow Freighter docked over there," Del says. "Protector shielding's got a similar build to the *Titania*'s. Made by same company. Might be some spare coolant packs. They won't fit exactly but—I could try—"

"Okay, okay. Let's go. Fast."

I wait just outside the freighter while Del searches inside. Xander and Rafiq are interrogating me over the comm link the whole time, panicked and afraid, asking what went wrong in there, what's going on.

"I can't even explain it."

"Mina? The captain's really gone?"

"He's really gone."

"Do you know how to fly the shuttle?"

"Fuck. Fuck."

"You don't?"

"I do. I know how. I've done all the training modules. I can do it." *I'll try.*

Del comes back holding a foil-coated duffel. "I found some stuff," he says.

"Let's go." We wriggle our way up the chute and into the shuttle. I strap into the captain's seat, Del beside me. We're both shaking. We've both forgotten how to breathe.

I ease the shuttle out of the hangar and past the membrane and toward the *Titania*.

***

The components we brought back aren't perfect, but Del works on the system with stopgaps and hacks and fixes it up enough to work for a few days.

The *Titania* is limping by the time we make it to Soline, but we make it. We deliver the cargo and earn our paycheck. It's a lot of money.

A *lot* of money.

We only spend a day on Soline. Just long enough to replace the damaged components on the ship, restock, refuel. We leave the colony as quickly as we can.

The ship is ours now. As long as we can stay ahead of whoever was after the captain.

We head for deep space, the unexplored outposts, the unknown worlds.

We delivered the cargo but something's stayed with us, too. Something remains.

***

Back on Soline, the carnage begins with blood and screams and fire.

It begins and doesn't end until there's nothing left but the burnt-out husks of buildings and smoking plastic and scarlet spattered across the snow.

And the cargo, of course.

It settles down to wait.

CONSENT

NANCY BAKER

The planes come in, running ahead of a freak desert electrical storm. Radios crackle with pleas and threats. From the exhaust trails, the subtle, sweet tang of blood and vengeance drifts down to touch the tarmac.

The airport lets them land.

"If they control our nightmares and dreams, they'll soon control our rational thoughts as well. It is our dreams—and our nightmares—that lead us to the truth, good and bad, of our humanity. It is our thoughts that give us the freedom we have waged wars to defend. If we surrender control of the expression of any of these things to someone else, then the true nightmare will have begun...."

The writer leans against the cold wall of the darkened hangar, hands bound to concrete blocks on either side, listening to his own voice from the tape deck on the floor in front of him. His head throbs from the blow to the back of it. His pride hurts more, for falling for the whispered promise of a private flight out of the strike-bound airport the storm had dumped him in, bribes to the controllers paid by an admiring fan. He remembers the walk across the deserted runway to the darkened hangar, automatically noting the particular and peculiar smell of the air, gasoline and desert mingling, and the way the dim lights behind him had laid pale ovals that never quite touched onto the tarmac ahead of him.

He searches for endings to this strange scenario and wishes for once he did not have such a vivid imagination.

Something moves from behind the shadowed bulk of a plane, steps into the circle of light cast by a work lamp lying on the floor. For a moment, all the writer sees is a column of darkness stooping by the tape deck. His voice dies and the black shape dissolves on the concrete.

He squints and it resolves itself in a human shape, draped and veiled.

"You were very eloquent." It is a woman's voice, soft, with the faintest edge of something dark and sharp beneath its gentleness.

He gropes for something to say, some response to unexpected praise for a speech he finished only hours earlier, sitting before the long row of senators on the dais. "Thank you," he says at last, when nothing else surfaces.

"I'm sure it doesn't hurt your sales either."

"I don't know about that. My books have been taken off shelves in a lot of bookstores and libraries." Three years had not changed that and every time he spoke out it happened again. Somewhere.

"But you still testified today."

"Of course. If they legislate everything I do and believe in out of existence, it won't be because I stood by and let them."

"You are very passionate about it."

"Of course I am. I'm defending my life, after all."

"No, Mr. Donovan, you are defending your livelihood. Not your life. I don't think you know anything about having to defend your life."

"Who are you?"

"My name is Katherine Wingate."

Her face, blurred by newsprint, flashes through his mind, memorable only because of the ones who had preceded her. And the calls from the Charlotte police wanting to discuss his books. He remembers a woman with long brown hair, brown eyes, average features. Ordinary-looking. Forgettable. If there have been pictures of her…after…he has not seen them. "What are you doing here?" he asks. Being stranded in an airport with this woman, of all the women in the world, is a coincidence so laughable he would be embarrassed to put it on paper.

"My plane followed yours from Washington."

"Your plane…" he echoes, trying to imagine this black heap on a commercial flight, stuffed into a too-small seat beneath the glare of the cabin lights, accepting foil-wrapped peanuts from a flight attendant.

"A private one," she answers, sensing his confusion. "Good Nite's Rest Motels settled out of court. I suppose their lawyers finally realized that a jury would only have to take one look at me to decide that their lies about their motel's security were to blame for…what happened."

He remembers a brief article two years ago, noted and thrust aside with the turning of a page. The headline flashes across his mind: Woodside Survivor sues Motel Chain for $10 million. He wonders briefly how much she got—but does not ask. There is only one question he needs answered. He finds the strength to ask it.

"Then what do you want from me?"

"The police killed Jonathan Heller. Good Nite's Rest Motels has paid. You're the only one left."

"I wasn't responsible for Jonathan Heller!" The words come out harsh and ragged, scarred by the memory of the Woodside Killer and the sad-eyed bank clerk he'd turned out to be. He feels a sudden pain in his wrists and realizes he has lurched forward, trying to escape.

"No? It wasn't your books he read? It wasn't your murders he copied?"

"Jonathan Heller was crazy. He'd been crazy all his life. He'd have been crazy even if all he ever read were the Saturday comics."

"Maybe. But the Saturday comics wouldn't have taught him how to kill. The Saturday comics wouldn't have given him reasons and justifications for it. You did. You and all the writers like you."

"We don't tell people how to behave. All we do is report on the darkness inside human souls; we report the evil we are capable of. We don't make anyone become that evil." He has said these words a hundred times in a hundred ways, for articles and debates and Senate hearings. Practice overrides panic and gives him answers that he suddenly wishes didn't sound glib and rehearsed, despite all his belief in them.

"'The blade slid in like it was a lost part of her, finding its way back inside, moving sweetly beneath the muscle and fat to touch the blackness inside. There was no blood, not with the silver hilt right up against her seamless skin. She screamed against the gag, eyes wide.'" Her voice is distant, distracted. "I memorized it, you see. He liked that passage. He would read it over and over while he tried to decide where the blackness in me was. It was from *Black Razor*. When he read, I could see your picture on the back cover, watching me. He'd already worked through *Red Night* and *The Watching Dark*. He was going to try to beat the killer's record of five days." There is a pause and he sees the veiled head lift a little. "Of course, he only made it to three with me before the police came."

"Ms. Wingate, I'm sorry about what happened to you. But what I write is fiction, just fiction. It's meant to entertain people, to give them a vicarious scare and to make them realize the dark side of our own natures. But it's never been meant to make anyone do what Jonathan Heller did to you and those other women."

"But that's what happened just the same. Because you told him it was all right. Your books and the movies and the magazines…they told him that it was just fine. We weren't real. We didn't matter. We weren't people. We were just things to use—and when that was done, we were just things to scream and bleed and die."

"I never…"

"No? 'Her eyes darkened and her throat fell back; the surrender of prey to predator, the consent of the deer to fall beneath the teeth of the wolf. He saw it over and over in the last moment—the willing yielding of their lives into his hands, the arch of their bodies onto the knife in voluntary ecstasy.'" She shifts to kneel, voice grinding out the words like broken glass.

"But in context…"

"Over and over again, you and all your friends tell them that it's all right, it's natural. The strong survive and weak surrender. The prey consents to be taken. The predator doesn't have to feel any guilt—it's the way of the world. But that's just the lie you tell to justify what you do—or what in your deepest soul you want to do. And it is a lie, Mr. Donovan. No one consents."

Her voice rises, her hands clutch at the dark cloth concealing her.

"Do you think I surrendered? Do you think I wanted it? Do you think I consented to this?"

Cloth tears and the veils fall away. He sees her white skin, ribboned in red scars. One breast is gone, the other is nipple-less. Angry, puckered lines drag her mouth into a sneer, wrap around her cheek and jaw and pull down one eye. Jesus, how had she survived, he wonders numbly. How had she endured it?

"Is it like you thought? When you were typing the words, is this what you saw? Did he get it right?" She spits the questions out sarcastically then draws the dark clothes over her burning white and red nakedness.

"I'm sorry, Christ knows, I'm sorry. But it wasn't my fault," the writer repeats desperately. Caroline's face flashes through his mind, standing beside his computer, reading the glowing words with a faint frown. He thinks of the killer and the room in the basement and words flowing like blood from his fingers and across the screen. Remembers the sharp, triumphant thrill of finding the perfect images, the perfect phrases, to express the visions flickering through his mind.

"It doesn't matter," she says softly, from behind the veil. "We can't change the past."

"No, we can't." He clings to the words, to the sweet rational sound of them.

"But I can't let you go on lying. I can't let you tell some other man how to kill." Her hand moves and something flashes against her darkness.

He pleads then, dragging up any argument he can find, from his wife and child to the legal and moral consequences of murder. But she can counter each of his future losses with her own past ones and brushes aside the promises of damnation and prison.

"I have five million dollars in a Swiss Bank account and a plane to take me away," she points out calmly, crouching beside him. "I bought a house in Tripoli. The Libyans won't extradite me. And I have grown quite used to wearing veils."

"I don't consent, damnit, I don't consent. I don't fucking consent!" He flings her own words back at her—but knows that his lack of consent means no more than hers did. For one last moment he wishes that his fictions were as true as Heller had believed, wishes that there could be some semblance of safety in surrender.

"Are you sure," she whispers and then the light breaks off the edge of the knife and blinds him.

***

The wheels of the jet roll across the slick tarmac. For a moment, the asphalt seems to suck at them, seeking to catch the plane and swallow it down into the tarry blackness.

In the dark hangar, something thrashes. If it had a tongue left, it might scream. If it had hands left, it might scrawl down the images of its dying in its own, best-selling style.

The blackness beneath the plane releases it.

The airport lets it go.

BRUJA

KATHRYN PTACEK

Chato Del-Klinne looked around at the airport terminal as he stepped out of the jetway. Not precisely Kansas, he could hear Sunny say teasingly as if she stood next to him, and he would have smiled, except he didn't feel like it; he felt…uneasy.

Not precisely Kansas, no.

Southern Texas along the Mexican border, to be more precise. He'd been asleep on the plane, thinking he was heading back to Las Vegas when the captain announced that because of the vigorous storm system to the west, he had been ordered to change his route and land at Dry Plains International instead of Dallas/Fort Worth.

"Vigorous." Chato shook his head. He just loved these euphemistic terms. Vigorous…meaning the entire western sky was painted a sickly yellow green, twenty twisters had been spotted between Dallas/Fort Worth and Amarillo, and if everyone was lucky, the tornados wouldn't remove the top six inches of soil throughout the state of Texas, not to mention every single trailer park in the Lone Star State.

And so here he was. The airport was bigger than he'd expected. It was, after all, an international airport, but mostly he had discovered with great irony that in the southwest that term meant flights scheduled to and from Mexico. Period.

International.

Yeah, right.

What he hadn't expected was the sheer chaos of the place. Many passengers milled around, while some clumped together to speak angrily about delayed or cancelled flights; somewhere someone was sobbing. Children darted back and forth, and several babies wailed.

He had the sense that something had happened, something horrible, and there was only one sort of thing like that that could make an airport chaotic. Yet the captain of Chato's plane had mentioned no disaster.

Maybe it just happened now. No, he would have heard something. So, it—whatever it was—had occurred before his flight put down. It must have been after the one announcement, and it was must have been too late for the pilot to go to another airport; jets had only so much reserve fuel, after all.

So, they didn't say a thing because they wanted to keep us from panicking, he thought grimly. Swell.

A youth hardly out of his teens and dressed in old jeans and a white T-shirt smeared with something dark walked by.

Chato grabbed the young man's arm. "Excuse me. What happened here, can you tell me? I just got off a plane from New York and—"

"A bomb!" the youth cried, his voice thick with fear and a West Texas accent.

"Where?"

The kid nodded with his chin toward the line of tall windows opposite the gate where Chato had disembarked. "Out there.

Some terrorist had a bomb. I think it was one of them Eye-ranians. Blew up the whole plane right there on the runway. It was terrible, just terrible. They got firemen and ambulances out there, but I don't know if anyone's gonna make it…" The kid began sobbing and Chato let go and watched as he struggled through the crowd.

Chato was stunned. A terrorist here? He moved forward, and looked out toward the line of windows on the left, and now he could see the wreckage in the distance, maybe a quarter of a mile. He saw emergency vehicles, and saw the flames and billowing black smoke, even in the daylight, and he wondered how his plane's pilot had negotiated the landing so that no one aboard had seen it.

Clever, real clever. Chato didn't much like being manipulated like that. Of course, what good would it have done to panic them while they were still in the air? Yeah, right; wait until we're on the ground, then we can panic.

Now, he watched as people scrambled along the tarmac, some into ambulances, others standing with emergency personnel; he sensed futility. No matter what they did out there…it was too late. Inside the building he watched as men and women and children stumbled along, some pushing others, all of them close to panicking. The bomb had set them off, too, he knew; maybe they were afraid that there were other terrorists, perhaps even in the building who might harm others.

Terrorists. In a border airport in southern Texas. Sure. Dallas-Fort Worth airport, yeah, maybe. But here? Something wasn't right.

He checked a monitor. Most departing flights were cancelled; his was one. Of course.

Someone next to him started complaining that when he got home he was going to write to the president of the airlines about this incompetence—he had important business in Vegas, by God, and it had to be done on time, by God—and Chato was relieved he wouldn't have to fly all the way to Nevada with him; with his luck, the guy would have sat next to him and bitched the whole time.

Now that he knew he didn't have to rush for a connecting flight, he took time to study his fellow strandees. They were a mixed bag: young and old and in-between, a few in wheelchairs or with canes, a fairly equal combination of Anglo and black and Hispanic, with a handful of Asians. Knots of businessmen in anonymous grey suits and look-alike leather briefcases, and several elderly nuns in old-fashioned habits, a Dallas matron with bouffant hairdo and too much eye makeup, a black kid with gold chains and a gold front tooth to match, two little girls in matching pink and lavender outfits each clutching a stuffed animal, a tall Sikh in all white, and more, dozens more. These people didn't seem to know where they were going, only that they didn't want to stay here, didn't want to stay in one place for too long. And beneath the anxiety and disorientation…

He felt…it.

He supposed he'd been vaguely aware of it before this; perhaps it was what had troubled him when he first arrived. But now that he stood there, not moving, he felt it, felt that touch of something else, of somewhere else.

He had had several close brushes with the supernatural before, and he knew its caress.

An Apache shaman, he'd trained with his teacher long ago before leaving home; for a long time he had turned his back on his discipline. But in the past few years he'd gone through a lot, and his instruction had come in handy.

There was more here than just the explosion out on the runway. God knows, that would have been enough for most places, but not here. There was more…much more.

Blood had been spilled here, he could smell it, and could sense, too, that something had awakened with the spilling of the blood.

He felt as if something shifted under his feet, but when he looked back he saw nothing but the innocuous grey tile.

Sunny, he thought suddenly. He had to get to a phone and let her know that he was okay. He checked his watch. 6:15 here, which meant 4:15 at home, and she'd be expecting him in a few hours. Only he wasn't going to be at McCarron in a few hours.

Mechanically he moved toward the phones, then stopped when he saw the lines there. They snaked back away from the handful of booths, back toward the waiting area.

Determined, he walked into another gate area, but the situation was the same there. At the newsstand no one stood behind the register. Several customers waited patiently to pay, if only someone would appear; one guy was busy reading the *Wall Street Journal*, not even aware of what was going on around him. Behind him a short Hispanic woman stood with a magazine in her hand.

As he studied the area, he realized that since he'd arrived he hadn't seen a single airport employee. No one manned the ticket desks at the gates, nor had there been any announcements about incoming flights or departures. There was nothing but the damned Muzak inanely playing some cheerful mishmash of a Beatles tune.

He had the feeling someone was watching him, but when he looked around he saw that everyone else seemed occupied in their own little drama. Still, he couldn't shake the feeling. The hair at the back of his neck prickled, and he rubbed the area. He tightened the band holding back his long black hair, then sighed.

Puzzled, he took the escalator to the lower level where the barrage carrousels were located. The carrousels moved, all right, going around and around, but no luggage shot out of the chutes. He checked the rental car desks; no one. No one stood behind the ticket reservation counters, either.

In fact, except for hundreds of panicked passengers the airport was deserted. He looked outside and saw no taxis waiting along the curb. There were no porters, either.

Where were all the airport employees? Off somewhere having a union meeting? On a mass coffee break, perhaps?

Or had they fled?

He thought he smelled burning french fries drifting down from the upper level, and he hoped that someone would go into one of the restaurants and investigate before the whole place caught on fire.

The music system was now playing "Raindrops Keep Falling on My Head." God, how he hated bouncy tunes like that. It was all so…pasteurized.

He went outside and winced as the oppressive heat of the Texas summer afternoon hit him. Then all at once he smelled the acrid fumes from the bombed airplane. He watched now as one of the ambulances he'd seen earlier swung around the building and shot out toward the highway. The vehicle abruptly began swerving back and forth; suddenly it flipped over onto its side and burst into flames. The second ambulance, following some distance away, stopped with a squeal of brakes, and the side and back doors flew open and the emergency crew raced away, just seconds before the vehicle exploded.

For a while Chato had thought about taking one of the rental cars—he couldn't call it stealing in an emergency situation like this—and getting the hell out of this weird place, but seeing what had happened to the two ambulances made him change his mind. Maybe it was just a coincidence, he told himself. And maybe not.

Maybe something didn't want anything or anyone leaving the airport area.

It wasn't a thought he wanted to contemplate for long.

He studied the countryside surrounding Dry Plains International. Well, whoever had named it had certainly gotten that name right. He didn't see anything except a flat brown expanse stretching off to the horizon, and above it a murky faintly blue sky, almost as if there was a haze. No mountains, no rivers or lakes, no buildings, no trees or bushes or strange cacti, no landmarks whatsoever. It was as if a tabletop had been swept clear and this airport plunked down in the middle. He had seen some desolate places, but man, this beat 'em all.

Comforting, he thought, real comforting. Just where the hell was this place?

To further increase his apprehension a dry hot wind howled around the corner of the building, and in the wind he thought he heard voices, strange voices that seemed to whisper his name.

Quickly he went back inside through the automatic doors before the electricity decided to go off and strand him outside. He wasn't sure which was worse: being stuck outside or in. As if something had read his thoughts, the lights overhead flickered momentarily, and somewhere there was a high-pitched scream.

He decided right then and there to go where there were people. Safety in numbers? he could hear Sunny tease him. Damned right, honey. This level was far too deserted for his liking. Again, he felt like something was watching him, but again when he looked around, he saw no one.

The escalator stopped halfway between floors, and he was getting ready to walk up the rest of the distance when it started up again, only this time it went backwards. He managed to turn around before he got to the floor, then stood and stared at the slow-moving steps.

Well, he'd take the stairs now. Damned if he go on an elevator or try the escalator again.

As he walked toward the staircase, he thought he heard a sound like a moan. He stopped. There was no one near the escalator. Still no one at the car rental desks or airline counters. All that was left were two doors, each with its bland symbol symbolizing a man and a woman. He entered the men's restroom first.

"Hello?"

No answer. He checked all the stalls. Nothing.

He went next door to the ladies' restroom.

"Hello?"

He heard a movement in one of the stalls, and pushed open the door which hadn't been locked. A young blonde woman—she couldn't have been much over eighteen, he decided—huddled there. A very pregnant young woman, he thought, when she shifted.

"Do you need help?" he asked gently.

She nodded. When she looked up at him, he could see that tears had left mascara smudges down her cheeks.

"Let me take you back upstairs where there are other people," he said.

"I-I think the baby's about to come. I came in here. I didn't know what else to do," the girl said.

"Maybe there's a doctor or nurse on the second floor," Chato said as he took her by the hand, easing her to her feet. She shuffled forward a few inches, then groaned. He realized she needed to lay down right away, but he would have to get her upstairs for that. Maybe they could break into the airlines' lounge. Surely they had couches in there.

But once he got the girl outside the bathroom and halfway to the escalator he realized they weren't going to get upstairs. She could barely hobble and kept crying the entire time.

While he had been looking around, he'd seen an area back of the stairs that made a protected nook. He took her there and told her to wait, then searched the lower level until he found a chair for her. She sank into it with a grunt.

"I need to go up and see if there's a doctor, okay?"

"No! Don't leave me!" She gripped his hand.

"Look, miss—"

"Gail."

"Gail," he said, trying to keep his tone reasonable. He needed to calm her, reassure her somehow that everything would be all right, when he wasn't at all sure himself that things would be all right. "It'll just be a few minutes. You're okay here. You've got this comfortable chair and—"

She squeezed his hand harder. "No, please, don't leave. I think someone's after me."

"No one can see you back here," he said. "It's out of the way. You can't be seen from the stairway or the doors or—"

"No, no, no! You don't understand. I've been hearing this voice ever since I got off the plane. Gail, it's been saying, give me your baby. I want your baby. I need your baby."

Chato stared down at her tear-streaked face, and knew then that this wasn't something she was imagining. She had heard the voice.

"Right. Okay. Look, give me a few minutes to scout around." He held up a hand when she started to protest. "I won't be long. But I want to see what I can find to make you more comfortable. Okay?"

She nodded.

"Just sit here and be quiet, and if anyone approaches…scream like hell, and I'll come running."

She nodded again, pressed a hand to her abdomen. "Thank you. You know, I don't even know your name."

"Chato."

He ducked out of the nook and glanced around the lower level. Empty as before. Or was it? The hairs along the back of his neck prickled again. Someone watched. He had thought that before. Now he knew he wasn't imagining it.

"Some Enchanted Evening" played on the music system.

That, he decided, could go off any time soon, and he'd be all the happier for it.

One airline counter over he found a door leading into an employees' lounge. Lots to loot here, he thought with a wry smile. He dragged the seat cushions from some couches back to the nook. He would have brought a couch, he explained, but he didn't think he could get it through the doorway.

"I'll be back," he said.

He returned to the lounge and found a closet full of the lap blankets that flight attendants give passengers, along with a dozen or more small pillows. He took everything there he could carry back to Gail. He tucked pillows around her, and covered her with the blankets, and stacked some nearby.

Just in case, he thought. Just in case when the baby comes, and I have to deliver it. He felt a spike of panic. His shaman training didn't include lessons in childbirth. This he'd have to wing.

He'd been aware for some time of more noise from above, and it sounded now like screaming and shouting and assorted bumping and scraping. He wondered what was going on, but he wasn't about to go and investigate. And he hoped whatever was up there wouldn't make its way down here.

Not for the first time he realized they were virtually trapped in the nook. The safe place could become in a moment's notice a prison.

But what choice did they have? He didn't want to settle her in the middle of the deserted level, where anyone—or anything—could see them.

He went scouting again and came back with two fire extinguishers. Not the best choice of weapons, he told himself, but when you have nothing else at hand. Well, that's not precisely true, he realized. He did have his Swiss army knife. Yeah, that would be a lot of use, wouldn't it? Besides, if he had smelled something burning earlier, these canisters might come in handy. If the electricity went off, he could always break the windows with them so they could escape outside.

He saw that Gail had fallen asleep, and so he sneaked back to the employees' lounge. When he saw the vending machines again, he realized just how hungry he had was. He had slept through dinner on the plane, and hadn't had anything since he'd left New York City that morning. And he knew Gail would be hungry.

He reached into his pocket for change, and thought, what the hell am I doing? He didn't have enough for two candy bars, much less what he knew they'd need.

He studied the first machine, one for sodas, then took out his pocket knife, selected a blade he thought would fit and inserted it and began jiggling it back and forth in the lock on the front panel. Finally he was rewarded with a snick, and the panel opened. He did the same for the other machines.

Something thudded onto the floor above and he half-expected to see someone or something falling through the ceiling. But it held. For now.

He located several empty cartons and put all the cans of soda in there, as well as dozens of packets of cookies and potato chips and cellophane-wrapped sandwiches and candy bars. He threw in what paper napkins and plastic cutlery he found; he opened all the drawers and doors he could find to see what other goodies he could liberate. When he left, he thought the room looked like locusts had swept through.

He winced. Somehow he didn't like the imagery.

When he got back, Gail was awake and had struggled up to a sitting position. He put the boxes down with the others he'd brought back earlier.

"Hungry?"

She nodded.

He pawed through the contents of a box. "I have ham and cheese, or ham and cheese, or ham and cheese." She giggled and suddenly she looked much younger than her eighteen years. "Or the ever popular ham and cheese."

"It's such a hard decision. Umm. Let me have the ham and cheese, please."

"An excellent choice. And what will you have to wash it down with? Here we have more choice. Clear soda, orange soda or brown soda."

"Orange, please."

Somehow he knew she would choose that. He opened the can and handed it to her. He was sitting on the chair now.

"I'll be back."

He went back to the airline counters and hunted around until he came to another fire alarm box. He took the fire axe. A better weapon.

On his way back he grabbed some pads of paper and pens. They might as well keep occupied while waiting for the baby.

He was heading back to the nook when he saw something on the now-stopped escalator. He edged closer. A thin trickle of blood dripped down from the floor above to the first tread of the escalator, crawled along the grooved metal plating, then dribbled down onto the tread below. Tread after tread, the blood dripped slowly down.

He backed away quickly.

"What's the matter?" Gail said, looking up from her sandwich when he came back.

"Nothing," he said with what he hoped was a steady smile.

"You're a bad liar," she said.

"I know. Sunny—my girlfriend—always says that."

He thought Gail seemed steadier now that she was eating and drinking something. Plus, he reminded himself, she wasn't by herself. That had to be a bit more reassuring, even if he didn't know what was going to happen.

"I don't know anything about you," he said after he finished his first sandwich and started on a second. He had never realized how good stale bread and dry cheese could taste. "You married?" She shook her head. "About to be?" She nodded. "And your boyfriend abandoned you, right?"

"Yeah, how did you know?"

"Lucky guess. Well, you're better off without him. He wouldn't have been much help now, I suspect."

"No, Randy said I was getting too fat and ugly."

"You're certainly not ugly. And you're not fat. You're pregnant. There's a big difference."

She flashed him a grateful smile.

"Where you going to?"

"Home to Omaha. I wanted to be with my family. My parents don't know about…my pregnancy. I guess my dad will yell a bit, but he really loves me, and my mom will just glare at him until he shuts up. It's the only place I can go. I was running out of money."

"Sounds like a good place, basically."

"What about you, Chato?" She was gnawing on her lower lip. She hadn't made any noise for some time, but he knew she was hurting.

"I live in Las Vegas; I was coming from New York City going through Dallas-Fort Worth, but got diverted here. I do odd jobs, I guess you could say, sort of this and that. Sunny is a blackjack dealer at a casino. What else? Well, I grew up in New Mexico."

"And you're Indian," she said softly.

"Yeah. Chiricahua Apache."

"I went to school with some Sioux. There are a lot of Indians in Nebraska, you know."

"Yeah, I know." He paused as he thought he heard someone speak. Hadn't they said Gail? No, it couldn't be. "Hey, I brought along some paper and some pens, and thought after we have our dessert of Paydays or Hershey bars, we could have a rollicking game of hangman. How's that sound?"

She winced slightly from pain. "Great. I think I'm ready for my dessert now. What were you doing in New York?" she asked as she peeled back the wrapper.

"Business. Okay. I was at some meetings in northern New York state."

"Are you an Indian activist?" she asked.

He was surprised by her question.

She smiled. "I heard about the protests up there with the Mohawks, and just wondered."

"Yeah, well, I was there at the same time, although for different reasons. I'm not really an activist, though." He didn't want to go into details of the matter that he had handled; he thought it would be too upsetting for her now. There had been some misunderstandings, some deaths; nothing was ever as easy as he thought it would be. He rubbed at a scar on his arm, an red angry-looking scar all too recent. He should know better by now; except that he didn't.

She sensed his reluctance and didn't pursue it. "How about that game now?"

"Fine."

He drew a hanging tree, and twelve spaces below it, then showed her the pad of paper.

"Twelve letters? Oh no! I was never good with long words!"

She had guessed eight of the letters when the really big pain shot through her, and she groaned so loudly he dropped the paper. He realized she'd been huffing her breath for the past few minutes, and he hadn't even noticed.

"Oh damn," he muttered when he saw her face, and leaped to his feet. The baby was coming.

Rolling up his sleeves as he dashed into the bathroom, he scrubbed his arms with soap and hot water, dried them, then came back to where Gail lay moaning softly.

He checked his supplies. He was as prepared as he'd ever be—rolls of paper towels, spare blankets, a bucket of water and sponges. Now, if he just knew how to deliver a baby, he'd feel a little happier about the situation.

He helped her lay back down on the couch cushions, settled a pillow beneath her head.

"Okay?"

She nodded, her breath huffing faster. She seemed to be counting silently. Then she said, "I have too many clothes on. You-you're going to have to help me."

He was embarrassed for himself and for her, too. He helped her remove her panties and push back her dress, and then he draped a blanket over her upraised knees.

Oh God, Sunny, he thought, where are you when I need you? He didn't know that Sunny had ever birthed a baby, but he wouldn't put it past her, and he knew she'd just stride into this little maternity cubbyhole, take in the situation at once, roll up her sleeves, and that would be that. Sunny would take care of everything.

Only Sunny wasn't here; he was.

"Oh God!"

Gail gripped his hand as he told her to push. That's what they did on TV, he told himself, so he assumed it was close enough to truth.

"Push again. That a girl. Good. Again."

The umbilical cord. What was he going to do about that? Oh Jesus, what had he gotten himself mixed up in? Then he remembered his pocket knife. He'd clean a blade off the best he could and he'd use that.

What if the baby died? What if Gail died? What if she bled to death right here? He'd have to go get help, he knew it. But upstairs…was there any help upstairs?

No. There was just him and Gail and a baby about to be born.

And almost before he knew it then the baby was coming, and he could see its head, and he told Gail to push harder and harder, and she screamed at him that she was, Goddamnit, and he told her she was doing good, really good, and then all at once there was a baby in his hands. A tiny warm thing covered with blood, and the wrinkled faced contorted itself, and he remembered some dumb medical show he used to watch, and he gently pried open the baby's mouth and removed mucus, and the baby coughed and started to cry.

Gail, her hair plastered dark against her forehead, smiled weakly. "Girl or boy?"

"Girl."

"Good. Boys are nothing but trouble. Does she have all her toes and fingers?"

"Sure does."

He cut the umbilical cord, and cleaned the baby gently with the paper napkins and towels, then wrapped her in one of the blankets. He had to clean up. And he had to help Gail clean up.

Still holding the baby, he stared down at her and she blinked up at him. He felt an inane urge to grin foolishly. Babies did that to people, he knew.

He heard a sound behind him.

A small white-haired woman stood there. It was, he realized, the woman from the newsstand.

"I will take over from here," she said softly, and her eyes were the yellow brown of a wolf's.

And he knew that this woman was part of the reason for his unease.

He knew in an instant what she was. Bruja. Witch.

Beyond her something shimmered, and at first Chato thought it was fog that had somehow crept into the terminal, but then he squinted and the fog coalesced. In the rippling light he could see figures that were there but not there, men from the past, dressed in feather headgear, cotton tunics and shields. Their dark bodies glistened as if oiled, and the men grinned fiercely.

"These are my ancestors," the woman said. "They suffered much under the whites. And they are hungry for their revenge."

Chato didn't have to ask how they would be brought into this time. He saw the bruja eyeing the baby, and he knew without question she would harm the newborn, would…sacrifice…it.

Not if he had anything to say about it.

Suddenly she leaped forward and grabbed the infant, and turned and ran.

"No!" Gail shrieked and tried to stagger to her feet.

"Stay there!" he yelled back at the girl as he raced after the woman. For someone so little, she certainly ran fast, he thought. He risked a glance back over his shoulder, and saw that Gail had obeyed and was back by the nook. Good. He didn't want to have to worry about her as well. God knew what else was wandering around this airport.

This part of the building had grown darker now, as if it were close to nighttime, yet Chato knew it wasn't. He glanced out the windows as he ran, and saw a gloom. But he didn't have time to think any more about it. He saw a door closing ahead, and knew the bruja had gone through it.

He stopped moments before he slammed into the wall, wrenched open the door and stepped through…

…and fell down a steep and rough slope. He tumbled and twisted and bounced, and once slammed his knee against a boulder. Finally, he came to a rest at the bottom. Puffs of dust rose around him, making him cough.

Nothing vital, he thought, was broken, although when he managed to get to his feet he knew he was bleeding in several places; certainly he was bruised, and when he touched his side with his fingertips, he winced. He thought he might have cracked a rib or two.

Swell.

And just where the hell was he?

He seemed to be in a tunnel, rough-hewn from rock and the earth. The ceiling wasn't high, and when he lifted his arm, wincing with pain from his ribs, he found he could touch the surface easily. He was not given to claustrophobia, but he would have liked it if the place were a tad more spacious. The walls were scarcely an arm's length away on each side. The air smelled of must, of rich loamy earth…like a newly dug grave.

The tunnel should have been pitch-black, but it wasn't. It was faintly lit, as though the earthen walls around him were phosphorescent. He scraped some of the dirt away, and his fingers glowed slightly. Quickly he wiped his hand on his jeans.

His eyes had adjusted to the semi-darkness now, and he could see that the walls weren't made of just dirt; objects seemed embedded in them. He stepped closer, and brushed away some grime so he could better see. He backed hastily away when he saw the gleaming white of a human skull. The matrix of the walls was human bones: skulls and femurs, shin bones, and the thin bones of fingers and toes. Here and there stiff hair and parchment-like skin clung. Here and there he could see a bas relief carved, images of skulls and skeletons and pyramids of bones.

He looked back up the slope, but couldn't see the doorway. There was no way out there; that much was obvious.

He would have to go down the tunnel.

He didn't want to go down the tunnel.

No choice, old pal, he told himself, and it almost sounded like he had spoken aloud, although he knew he hadn't.

Something brushed by his ear, and he shook his head.

The floor, he realized then, was made up of crushed bones. Inside his boots his toes curled, but he had no choice. He had to walk upon the dead.

Carefully he moved forward, suspicious there might be some trapdoor waiting for him; but the ground seemed solid enough. For now.

He noticed masks suspended from some of the walls. Intricately carved images that leered or glared down at him with the countenances of stern-faced warriors and eagles and reptiles and pumas and other feral beasts. Masks with elongated earlobes, exaggerated noses and lips, eyes that were narrow slits, tear-shaped or round as if with surprise. Masks hewn of coconut husk, of wood, of copper and silver and tin. Some had elaborate headdresses in turn, those the visages of jaguars and parrots. Bright feathers and plaits of human hair and strands of beads and teeth and shell dangled from the masks, and he saw the glint of gold and precious stones in the rings in the ears.

More light came from ahead, and he reached an opening on the right. There was a smallish room that seemed empty, and when he stepped into it, he saw himself as a boy of fourteen when his father had taken him to Ryan Josanie. His old teacher, the man who had taught him to be a shaman.

Josanie was showing the then-Chato how to control his dreams, and the youth was complaining that it was hard, and Josanie, not smiling, was saying that everything worth having is hard, and the then-Josanie glanced up and saw the now-Chato.

"Josanie." Seeing the old man brought him such sadness and regret. His teacher had been dead for years. Chato took a step forward, and with a shimmer, as it if were simply an image in water, the scene disappeared, and he was standing in an empty room.

He went out into the tunnel, which now turned to the left. Sometimes, he thought, the eyes of the skulls in the walls seemed to watch him, but he dismissed that thought. He was just getting spooked; that was all. Nothing was watching him.

Or was it.

He encountered another room. There he saw himself and Ross, his brother younger by three years, and they were at a state championship football game, and the then-Chato was in uniform, and Ross was saying how much he admired his brother, and Chato was laughing and telling he'd know better when he got older, and Ross saying he'd always respect his brother. Ross…whom he'd not seen in years, hadn't talked to for more than a year. Ross…they'd been close once. Now they had drifted so far apart.

Once again Chato took a step forward, and once again, the image, as if mirrored on the surface of water, disappeared.

Out in the tunnel he grew aware again of a sound that had

been with him since he'd entered this stygian world. Its rhythm was regular, he realized, and he thought it might be water dripping somewhere. No, more than that. And he recognized it then as the sound of a heart beating, and whether it was his or something else's he didn't know.

Some yards away he found another room, and this time he saw his mother and father working, working hard as they had always done to make a better life for his brother and him. They never complained, even though they often held down as many as two or three jobs at once, all so that their boys could go to school, would not live in the desperate poverty which they had known all too well.

In still another room he saw himself at the university, saw himself getting his degree, saw his parents in the audience, and he knew their pride. He was the first in the family to go beyond high school. He was proud, and yet he felt as if he had lost something that night, something of his people, and he didn't know what.

In yet another room he saw a woman he had loved long ago; they had parted amicably enough; and then he saw his old house in Albuquerque where he had lived when while a professor of geology there, and he remembered all the good times he'd had then, all the good friends he'd left behind long ago, all the memories that he had stepped away from.

Another chamber contained niches carved deep into the earth, and in the niches lay mummified bodies. Bodies that had been dead for decades, for a century or two or even longer. The dust was thick in this room, and he did not step inside. He feared to. Here and there he could see a scrap of cloth still sticking to the leathery skin of the mummies, and the air smelled faintly of herbs. Something moved opposite him, and he watched a centipede crawl out of one of the body's eyes.

His stomach rebelled, and he hurried away.

The path twisted to the right, and he stepped into a room and saw a man on a bed. The man was naked, and a blonde woman, equally exposed, sat astride him and ground her hips and moaned. Her hair was plastered in long sweaty strings down her back. The man on the bed reached up and brutally squeezed her breasts, and she cried out as she arched her back, and then she swiveled her head around and leered at him, and Chato saw with horror that the woman was Sunny.

"No!" he screamed. He stumbled from the room, and when he glanced back it was dark. No, no, no. Sunny wasn't with a man, wouldn't be; she loved him. Or did she? one part of him slyly whispered. She did, she did, she did. He repeated it to himself as if it were a mantra.

He rubbed his hand across his face, felt the sweat and grime there, and knew then that what he had seen was false. He had been misled, deliberately. Whoever—whatever—was doing this wanted him to lose heart, wanted him to give up.

But he wouldn't.

He took a deep breath, and followed the curve of the tunnel which was now heading downward slightly, and he wondered how far below the airport he was now. If that was really where he was.

Abruptly the tunnel ended, and there before him stretched a pool of water. He edged closer and saw reflected only himself.

Now what? he asked himself.

He inspected the wall beyond the water, the walls alongside him. Were there hidden doors somewhere? No. He knew that this was the way.

But if he jumped in, he would drown. Who knew how deep this was? He might just sink like a stone, and that would be the end of him. Or perhaps there were…things…slimy things waiting for him beneath the water, things that would suck the very breath from his body, and crush him with their rot-encrusted tentacles.

No, no, he couldn't do it. He had to go back, had to find another way to rescue the baby.

No, said a voice in his mind, and he knew it was old Josanie. Think.

He studied the water's tranquil surface. Nothing seemed to move below it. Nothing disturbed it.

Taking a deep breath, Chato took one step into the water and sank and sank and sank until he thought his lungs would burst from lack of oxygen, and then suddenly he was in another room, this one much larger than those lining the tunnel.

Firelight flickered, casting elongated shadows, shadows that seemed almost to move as if they were alive.

And there beyond the blaze stood the bruja, and she held the baby by its tiny heels, and dangled the child over the flames. The baby wailed miserably, and flailed its arms uselessly.

"You will pay," the woman whispered, and in that moment he saw she was not an old woman as he had first thought, but that her skin was dark and mottled, like that of a lizard, and her teeth were long and yellowed, something red staining them. From her back arched wings of jade and ebony feathers, feathers that moved, from the lice and maggots that crawled across them. She looked like a feathered serpent.

He blinked, but the image stayed the same, and in that moment, he saw she wore his mother's face, then that of Sunny, then that of a girl whom he had known long ago at the university, and then it was the face of the old woman, but only as she must have been long long ago. She was at once beautiful and terrible to see, and he saw now that she was completely naked except for the necklace of bones draped across her full breasts, and her bronzed skin gleamed.

She smiled at him, and beckoned to him with one hand, and in that hand he saw an obsidian knife.

He remained rooted where he was.

Her skin was tattooed. At least he thought they were tattoos. Tattoos of eyes, like the masks in the tunnel: mere slits, round, tear-shaped, and then with growing horror, he realized the eyes were watching him and that some had winked.

The woman's smile broadened. She raised her arm, the knife rising, and now he watched as the dagger came hurtling down and—

Without thinking, he threw himself across the fire. He was only dimly conscious of the sparks singeing his hair, burning his face and hands, and he grabbed the baby just as the knife slashed downward and pain shot through him as the obsidian cut through his sleeve into his flesh, and he yelled, and kicked out, and his boots connected with the woman, and she screamed as she lost her balance, and fell into the fire.

He scrabbled to his feet, the child cradled tightly in his arms, and watched as the woman writhed and howled as the flames licked up and down her body, melting the flesh away as it if were nothing more than thin tissue paper, and he watched as her bones burned, watched until there was nothing more than charred matter. Abruptly the fire died down, and there was only embers and what had been left of the bruja.

Tentatively he touched one of lumps with the toe of his boot, and he thought he could hear a faint cry.

He hurried away from the fire, then examined the room. It was elongated, the now-dead fire at one end, a pool of water at the other. He had come down before. Would he have to go down again? It didn't make sense. After all, he wanted to go up, but then maybe none of this made sense, at least as far as the rules of science went. This was a matter of something much darker, much older than science, after all.

The baby was whimpering, and he tried to shush her, but he knew she must be scared and hungry, and with a prayer that this was the right thing, he jumped into the water, and suddenly he was bobbing up and up and up through clear water, and his head broke the surface and he scrabbled out of it before the baby could drown.

Once more he was standing in the tunnel, and as far as he could see there was still no exit. It looked like he'd have to head up that slope. There was no way around it.

He clasped the infant closer to him and started toward the slope. He ignored the rooms on either side of him; he wanted to see nothing that they held. The walls seemed to grow closer upon him, and things with long plucking fingers reached out and grabbed at his tattered shirt, his burned skin, and he gritted his teeth against the pain.

Finally he came to the slope. He started climbing up, holding the baby with one hand, helping himself find a purchase with the other hand.

What if, he wondered halfway up, what if he got to the top, and he didn't see a doorway, just like when he fell down the slope.

Believe, one part of his mind said, and it was his voice, though, not Josanie's.

He reached the top, and rested, but there before him was the door. He pushed it open and stepped through, and he once more in the airport terminal, and when he glanced around, there was only a smooth wall.

He hurried toward the nook, afraid now that he would find Gail gone, but she was there, sitting on her bedding. She leaped to her feet when she saw him and rushed over, and he handed the baby to her.

"What happened to you?" she asked.

He knew how he must look. His hair was partly singed, some of it laying in wet strands across his cheek and forehead. His face and arms were bruised, he had blood and cuts and dirt all over him, not to mention the burns and scorchmarks.

He grinned.

"It's a long story." He took a deep breath and felt the sharp pain in his ribs; he had forgotten about them during all this; now he was very much reminded. "I think I'm going to wash up as best I can in the bathroom, and then I think we ought to get the hell out of here. You agree?"

She nodded. "I agree."

When he came out of the bathroom a few minutes later, he found she'd made a makeshift bed for the baby from a small carton, and that she'd packed some of their things—mostly the food and drink and blankets—into a few other boxes.

"I didn't know how far we'd have to walk," she said.

"Walk? Hell, we're going to drive," he said, and he strode over to one of the rental car stations, and grabbed a handful of keys. "We're going to go to the rental lot, and find what fits where, and when we do, we're getting in and not looking back." He didn't mention the vehicles that he'd seen earlier, the ones that couldn't get out of the airport. Not now.

He wasn't about to stop for anyone or anything now, not after what he'd just gone through.

It took them half an hour but they found a blue T-bird, and got their boxes settled in. Gail strapped herself in, then held the baby tightly.

Chato got behind the wheel, put on his seatbelt, adjusted mirrors and seat, and turned on the car, and without thinking, flipped on the turn signal. He grinned when he realized it wasn't necessary. Old habits.

Then they drove out of the deserted rental car lot, and into the outbound lane, and when they reached the shells of the ambulances, he saw that Gail started to shake as she realized what had happened earlier, and he said, looking into the rearview mirror and seeing the dark eyes of old Josanie, "I believe."

Chato drove away from the airport, away from the fire and the death, and it was only when they had driven over twenty miles further that he remembered he never had picked up his luggage. He began laughing.

That was okay. He's pick up some more bags. After all, he told himself as he looked over at the sleeping mother and child, luggage was cheap; life wasn't.

I AM NO LONGER

NANCY KILPATRICK

I am not the same woman I used to be. Events alter all of us. Sometimes irrevocably.

This journal began the day they delivered the computer. It's been a slow agonizing process, practicing for hours, hitting the modified keyboard with a touch stick clamped between my teeth. The spot where my jaw is hinged still aches much of the time, as do the muscles at the side of my neck, but I've got the hang of it. Those areas of my body are strong.

The computer is essential. It's vital that I write everything down. Somebody has got to keep a record; I have to keep a record. For now I have nothing else to do.

I never dreamed I'd end up in a place like Dry Plains. On the other hand, no nightmare ever warned I'd be paralyzed from C-7, the seventh vertebra down, my voice box severed in the six-car pileup outside Houston. That the newly conceived fetus inside me would be miscarried. That I'd spend the rest of my life talking to myself and what's left of the world through modern technology, the same technology that used to confuse and annoy me. But then I've come to understand and accept many things recently. I'm not the person I was.

By the time the hospital sent me home, the bills had piled to the ceiling and Terry was at his wit's end. The recession hit the factory where he was a manager. Recent trade agreements had taken a lot of work to Mexico. The baggage handler job in Dry Plains was all he could find. At least the bungalow near the airport was cheap.

Terry's life insurance paid off the mortgage. And bought the computer. I need the computer to keep Terry's truth alive. He knew what was going on at the airport. About all the 'accidents.' The flights where more passengers disembarked than the plane held. About the Indians. I'm one-quarter Comanche myself. On my mother's side. Maybe that's why I believed him. Now I believe him for other reasons.

I had a premonition of Terry's death. I get feelings. Always have. Like my grandmother. My vision blurs, I hear echoes. Sometimes a headache slices into the middle of my brain. Before the accident, my backbone used to feel as if someone had rammed an icy steel rod down it.

I tried to tell him: Don't go! You're in danger! Back then I only had the letter board and pointer to spell out a warning. It was tedious, I was always frustrated, the stick in my mouth, fumbling to point to the right letters, Terry having to figure out the words and then make sentences. He was endlessly patient, but that night he was late for work. He only got half the message: Don't go!

He paused at the door in his midnight-blue coveralls and looked at me with eyes brown as fertile soil that always reminded me of the harvest back on my grandmother's farm when I was a girl. Of plenty. Of happier times. What I couldn't say with words, I told him with my eyes. His turned fearful. "Got to go, Meg," he said, covering it up with forced cheerfulness. He kissed my mouth with his generous lips and smiled, his teeth so white, one chipped. The scent of musk from his aftershave lingering. "Rosanne rerun's on tonight. Why don't you watch it?" The door closed. I remember the cold empty feeling in the house; I swear I felt that rod up my spine.

His kiss left an invisible imprint on my lips; it caressed my skin through half the night, that and the tears coating my cheeks.

It was late when the world exploded. Even the dead must have felt the bomb tear up the runway. It was as if the earth had been slashed to the core. Hell fire shot skyward until the flames licked heaven's gate. The house grew frigid. I knew the moment Terry left the earth; the scent of musk vanished. His body was never found. That night I changed again.

Soon I started seeing them. Before they'd been just rumors. Talk Terry brought home from the airport. He didn't tell me, of course. He wouldn't have wanted to frighten me. I overheard him talking to his buddies. About the passenger who died of a sudden heart attack and then, two hours later, got up and walked, shoe soles not making a sound as they contacted the floor, skin too grey and mottled to be called living. About the red-headed Mexican twins, children really. They followed a black woman and her daughter from Atlanta into the washroom. And never came out. Two bodies were found, one adult, one teenage, the skin stripped off the way a hunter peels the hide from his prey to get at the carcass. Stories about hideous babies with yellow eyes and red teeth, who resembled stone demons, who sucked blood from engorged nipples. About half a dozen old men who carried tomahawks into the smoke shop, hacked the attendant to pieces, scattered tobacco all over the tarmac... And all the while it was business as usual at the airport.

I heard the stories and believed them. And now I see the spirits myself. Just like my grandmother used to. All day and all night. They roam the fields surrounding the airport, passing the house.

One paid me a visit. That's how I know they're ancestors. And how I know they are not wholesome spirits. They aren't here to help but to punish. For deeds long forgotten. To exact revenge on the sons of the fathers, and their sons. And the mothers and their daughters.

"I am Tacomaak." He said that without opening his mouth, our brains like two modems, connected. There was something hollow-looking about him yet sturdy. He was solid enough to break down the door all by himself but he could walk through walls, which I suspect is how he got inside my house. Maybe, in the past, I'd have been scared. But that part of me dried up and blew away with the parched earth of this desolate place. In my new widow's grief, I transmitted the message: Why are you here? Why now?

He was two heads shorter than me when I'd been able to stand. Dirty skin and hair, prominent nose and cheekbones slick with sweat stinking of mesquite. Maniacal black eyes glared through me, reflecting distorted images from the spirit land he came from. He knew I was paralyzed but I doubt he'd have found me a threat even if I could defend myself. From the way he stood rooted to the earth, I knew he didn't feel threatened by anyone.

Right away I sensed he was Comanche, although I can't say how I knew that. My mother did not like to talk about our native blood. I've seen movies, though. He was dressed warrior-fashion, fierce ochre and red clay face-paint, natural leather headband, a tomahawk and stone knife hanging from a beaded belt decorated with what I believe were scalps. Thick swatches of hair dangled in a row, shades of brown. One blond. Like Terry's. Dried blood clinging to it. Staring at those blood strands and then into Tacomaak's eyes, suddenly I understood everything. The bomb had not killed Terry. I knew why he had come here.

Any dry dust motes of emotion that remained in me were

moistened by my tears. They quickly turned into a mud slide that swallowed me. I never would have imagined myself pleading, but I did, in thought. He showed no mercy. His sharp knife gouged deep into my chest over my heart. It was not a wound that leads to death but a calculated mutilation of pure savagery. His mouth clamped onto my breast. Physically I could not feel his obscene kiss, or the brutal rape of my disabled body that followed—for that I am grateful to any benevolent spirits who may still exist. But physical pain is not the worst kind. Loaded into my cellular memory banks was an image. For a second two faces superimposed one over the other. A glitch. Mesquite and musk clogged my nostrils. I became irreversibly numb.

Generous lips smile. White teeth, one chipped. Smeared with red gore. Blazing hatred in inhuman eyes scorches me. He despises my mixed blood even as he greedily steals it.

***

I am not the same woman. I cannot feel the twisted thing growing inside me but I sense its coiled, warped energy draining my life force. My existence is a flat computer graphic. RAM memories keep me alive: a blond man who loved me with all his heart; my grandmother who blessed me. I am driven. I must delete something. If I do not, who will?

When the reincarnated demon crawls from my womb like a maggot, I will drive the plastic touch stick I have sharpened into its callous heart. And if I fail, if my body expires as this malevolent being seizes life, you who read this must act.

Do not be fooled—the spawn is not human. It is no friendly ancestor returning to guide us in our time of great need. It has come to destroy us. All of us.

Kill it!

I write this easily and with absolute certainty. The word mercy is not in my program.

I am no longer the person I once was.

FACELESS

SHANNON LAWRENCE

"**T**his is what we refer to as a spaghetti bag."

Pausing in her attempt to put her shoes back on, Delilah jerked her attention up to the airport security agent standing on the other side of the stainless steel surface. His military precision haircut framed a slightly pudgy visage, the beginnings of a five o'clock shadow on his cheeks and chin. Spaghetti bag? Was that a new terrorist term? "Pardon?"

"You've got all these cables in here. Spaghetti, you know? I'll need you to follow me so I can go through it."

With a sigh, Delilah followed the blue-shirted back of the agent. Around her, the hushed sound of voices hummed along in chorus with the moving security belts. The inside of her head felt stuffed with cotton from the dulled edges of sound and bright lights pulsating around her.

Happily, it was decided she wasn't a terrorist, merely a geek, and she zipped up her bag and headed toward the tram. An escalator took her down into a shiny tunnel, one wall full of ads, the other windows. She stopped in front of a giant sliding glass door and set down her bag, relinquishing the handle of her rolling suitcase while she waited with everyone else for the tram that would come shortly. Using the glass as a mirror, she straightened her tan skirt and adjusted her cream top. Her auburn hair was a mess, but all she could do was shift it around with her fingers in an attempt to shame it back into place.

Someone stepped up close behind her, and she looked into the window's reflection. She saw a dark halo of hair surrounding a blurry void, no visible facial features. With a jolt, she turned to look at the figure behind her and found a perfectly normal woman, almond-shaped eyes meeting hers for a brief moment. Delilah gave her a half smile and turned away, shaking her head at the odd jolt of panic she'd felt at seeing the featureless reflection.

A rumble began in the tunnel, followed by a red tram that whooshed along in front of Delilah. She watched the blur of faces as they coursed by her until the tram came to a stop. A ding sounded, followed by a calm, semi-metallic woman's voice.

"Please stand behind the red line until the doors open and the passengers depart."

She picked up the bag, securing it on her shoulder, and grabbed her suitcase handle. Another ding sounded and the door slid open, unleashing a torrent of dead-eyed tourists and business travelers from the guts of the tram. The scents of perfume and sweat washed over her as she waited her turn. A short, angular man jostled her as he moved by, his shoulder hitting her square in the breast.

"Excuse me!" she said, rubbing at the sore spot left behind. He didn't so much as look at her.

With an irritated grunt, she stepped onto the tram, too late to get one of the seats. She grabbed the nearest pole and leaned her suitcase against her leg. A stocky man came up to stand beside her, his meaty fist clenched around the pole just above her hand.

A smell like bologna wafted off him, and she thanked her lucky stars it wasn't worse.

She blew out a frustrated puff of air and held tighter as the tram began to move with a jerk, knocking the man's armpit against the side of her head. Like the previous guy, he didn't bother to apologize, and she made a point of staying as far from him as she could while they were wrapped around the same smooth piece of metal.

Staring into the car after theirs in an attempt to avoid looking at her pole-partner, Delilah ran her eyes over the passengers. Most wore bland expressions, their journey having only begun. A family chattered with animation, two kids holding tiny backpacks.

Her gaze drifted over a couple, both faces blurred, features indistinguishable. When she shot her eyes back to them, they looked completely normal. Man, I must be more tired than I thought. She shook her head and looked down at the ground, closing her eyes for a moment to rest them.

She listened, eyes still closed, as the tram screamed along the tracks, a whoosh signifying each metal brace they passed. Someone to her right coughed, sudden and sharp in the quiet car.

Shifting slightly, she looked in the other direction, staring through the large rectangle of plexi-glass that made up the window at the front of the car. In the next car, there was only one person. A woman stood directly in the center of it, staring back toward Delilah. She wore a well-cut red coat with black buttons and a black skirt that ended just above her knees. Despite the dim light of the tram, she wore giant sunglasses, Audrey Hepburn style, her dark hair pulled back into a tight topknot. Her chin was tilted down, and it was impossible to tell where her eyes rested. Was she actually looking at Delilah, or had something else caught her attention? Delilah turned her head to look behind her, but found nothing of interest, at least not that she could see.

When she turned back around, the woman still appeared to be staring at her, but her head had tilted to the side like a dog studying something interesting. Delilah braced herself and stared back, lips pressed together, forehead crinkled in indignant concentration.

The woman's head straightened. Was it Delilah's imagination or had a slight smile appeared on the woman's face?

With a jerk, the tram halted. The vaguely feminine robot voice filtered through the car: "Welcome to Terminal A. Please gather your items and step from the car. This is the end of the line."

Delilah looked down to grab her suitcase handle more fully, and when she looked up, the woman was gone. She held back, not eager to run into her in the brightly lit hallway outside. Better to let her get ahead. Her back crawled at the thought of the creepy way the woman had stared at her. Studied her.

She'd taken too long to get off the tram, and now people were crowding on. Exiting was like swimming upstream, and she found she had to put out an arm to ward off those coming at her. An elbow hit her in the ribs. A suitcase rolled over her foot. Everyone stared straight ahead, airport zombies with no interest in what stirred around them.

By the time she got out into the hallway, there were only a few stragglers. They headed off to her left, and she followed, assuming they knew where they were supposed to go. Lord knew she didn't. An escalator led up into the roaring terminal, and it was as if she'd stepped through an invisible barrier as a wall of sound hit her. The brrrr of rolling wheels surrounded her, battered by hundreds of voices, the tromp of feet. Somewhere, an infant cried. The scent of food enticed her, her mouth watering as she passed a fast food burger joint. When she walked past a bar, the hoppy smell of beer tickled her nose, voices louder here than the rest of the terminal.

A group of people milled about up ahead, and she paused to look at the digital sign hanging from the ceiling. ATLANTA scrolled past in red pixelated letters. This was it.

Taking a seat on the row of chairs along the main walkway, furthest from the check-in desk, Delilah unzipped her bag and pulled a book out. She tried to block out the sounds around her, but found she couldn't ignore them enough to get into the book. When she slid it back into the bag and looked up, the woman in the red coat stood a couple feet in front of her, still wearing those sunglasses. Her face was a blur behind them, and when she slid the glasses off her face, a void was left behind.

This time there could be no doubt. Delilah was looking directly at her, and the face was still a blur. They stared at each other this way, still as statues, until a man walked between them. Delilah blinked. And before her stood the woman, eyes so dark they were black, blood red lipstick on full lips that smiled, but only slightly.

Delilah leapt up from her seat and stepped toward the woman, who only watched, face unchanging.

"What is your problem?" Delilah asked, moving into her space.

The woman didn't answer, only looked back at her. This time when the woman cocked her head to the side, it felt sarcastic, one of her eyebrows quirking up just so, which only served to aggravate Delilah more.

"I'm asking you a question," she hissed, voice low as she tried to avoid making more of a scene. People around them were looking, faces open in curiosity. "Why do you keep staring at me?"

There was still no answer, and Delilah stood there a moment longer, hands fisted at her sides. She let out a frustrated breath and turned away to grab her things. As she picked them up, she turned once more to the woman and said, "Leave me alone or I will go to security."

***

Twenty minutes later, Delilah drained the last of her wine and set the glass on the shiny black counter. It had to be about boarding time now. She'd relaxed in the bar with no further issues, but she had to get back to the boarding area.

She picked up her bag and grabbed the handle of her suitcase, walking quickly, her heels tap-tapping along the hardwood floor of the bar until she reached the carpeting, which muffled her steps and the sound of the suitcase wheels.

There was no sign of the woman in red in the boarding area, and Delilah slipped into the growing line. The flight attendant took her boarding pass and slid it through a machine, handing it back. The gangway was cold as she stepped through the door, and Delilah walked down the slope, cool air slipping inside her coat.

At the bottom of the gangway, she ran into the back of the line again, and they stood there, shuffling their feet in the cold, more people piling up behind her. The man in front of her wore a navy blue suit jacket with tan pants. A white thread stuck to the back of the blazer, and it gnawed at Delilah. She looked down to study her boarding pass, avoiding looking at him, but she could see the thread out of the corner of her eye. Finally, she reached forward and gently pinched the thread between her fingers, pulling it off the soft material. He turned to look at her, and she mumbled, "Sorry, there was a thread." She held it up, proof that she didn't just poke random strangers. His eyebrows gathered above the bridge of his nose in a puzzled look, but he turned forward and didn't look back at her again, which was good enough for her.

Finally through the door, she put her suitcase in the overhead bin and stuffed the bag under the seat in front of her, settling into the aisle seat. The other two seats to her right were empty, so she knew she'd be standing back up to let her neighbors through. She drummed her fingers on the cool metal armrest and waited.

As soon as her seatmates, a middle-aged man in a polo shirt and khakis and a man in his twenties wearing jeans and a cocky smirk, were settled next to her, she buckled her seatbelt and leaned back against the headrest, closing her eyes. She felt it when someone sat in the seat in front of her, as the cushion pressed back into her knees, but she didn't open her eyes. People continued to bustle past her, clicks sounding around the cabin as overhead compartments were closed. A flight attendant walked past, steady professional pomp, pomp, pomp as her sensibly heeled shoes met the thin carpeting. Delilah half listened as she spoke quietly to people, helping them stow their items and find their seats. Voices mumbled around her in a steady rumble. The gentle scent of the middle-aged man's cologne wafted into her nose then receded, exposing her sinuses to the odd canned-air scent of the plane.

***

The ding of the seatbelt sign ripped Delilah out of her doze. She sat up, checked her seatbelt, and rubbed her eye with a knuckle. When she looked over, the middle-aged man gave her a gentle smile and looked down at the glossy trifold in his hands. She grabbed her own from the seatback in front of her and looked up at the flight attendant who stood in the aisle ahead. She could only see the flight attendant from the eyes up, as the person in front of her wore a high bun that stuck up above the seat, so she leaned over into the aisle and watched her giving instructions on exiting the plane, fastening seatbelts, pulling down gas masks, and using seats as flotation devices. When the flight attendant finished, Delilah realized she hadn't heard a word. Ah well, would she really have remembered all that information in the middle of a plane crash?

"Flown before, I take it?" The middle-aged man looked at her with an amused expression on his face, mouth quirked into a half smile.

"Yes. Why do you ask?"

"I always know a first-time flyer by the way they listen intently to the instructions and follow them with a finger on the pamphlet. It didn't look like you were actually listening."

Delilah laughed and said, "You caught me…?" She paused and raised her eyebrows.

"John."

"You caught me, John. Fly a lot?"

He nodded and stuffed his trifold into the seatback in front of him. Delilah did the same, and they settled back to await takeoff. The flight attendants moved to somewhere behind them, and it was only a few minutes before the airplane jerked to a start, reversing slowly.

It seemed to take forever to get to the runway, and then again for the plane to start forward. Then engines roared, and she was pressed back into her seat. John offered her a stick of gum, and she took it with a smile, unwrapping it and sticking it into her mouth as they lifted off. It felt like her stomach was lifting up into her chest, and then they were leveling off, white drifts of cottony clouds moving past the little oval windows.

Static broke out over the intercom, preceding the captain's voice. "We are now at a cruising altitude of 35,000 feet. You are welcome to remove your seatbelts and move around the cabin, but we recommend staying in your seat with your seat-belts buckled unless you need to use the restroom. Skies are clear ahead of us, and we should be landing in Atlanta at ten p.m. Eastern Time."

Despite the recommendation, the rampant click of seatbelts being removed rang throughout the cabin. Immediately, a man two rows up, on the other side of the aisle, stood up and stretched, stepping into the aisle and looking around. Delilah shook her head and leaned forward to mess with the buttons beside the small screen in the seat ahead of her to get a movie started. Earphones plugged in, she didn't stir until a flight attendant—her nametag declared her as Suzette—arrived with the drink cart.

Plastic cup and cellophane packet of pretzels in hand, Delilah watched as Suzette moved up to the seat in front of her. The bun moved as the woman wearing it looked up at the cheerful blonde flight attendant. A hand with cherry red nail polish reached over and touched Suzette's arm, and her face blurred, the features disappearing into a flesh-colored void. The blonde hair framing where her face should be turned in Delilah's direction.

Delilah gasped and pressed back into her seat, hands grasping the armrests. When she blinked to clear her eyes, Suzette was back to normal, moving up to the next row of seats, and the bun was back in its upright position.

"Are you all right?" John placed a gentle hand on hers, covering the whitened knuckles that strained against her skin.

"Yes, I'm okay. I wasn't feeling great all of a sudden, but it passed. Maybe I'm just hungry."

"Well, I hope you brought a snack of your own. Cheapskate airlines don't provide meals anymore unless you're flying a crazy number of hours." He shook his head and took a drink of his coffee.

"Maybe these will fill me up." She held up the packet of pretzels, earning a polite laugh from him.

She turned the volume up on her movie, drinking her juice and munching on the seven pretzels she'd fished out of the packet. Her eyes kept darting to the flight attendant as she made her way down the aisle, but her face didn't change again, and Delilah relaxed, working out the plans for her arrival in Atlanta. She still had a ways to go once she landed; a two-hour drive in a rental car would get her to her sister's place. By then, she'd be ready to fall into a nice, clean bed for a bit of sleep.

The light began to dim outside, pink touching the sky. Delilah took her headphones off and removed her seatbelt, slipping out of her seat. She looked around for the bathroom, saw the closest was behind her, and walked toward it. As she reached for the handle, she noticed the red "OCCUPIED" sign and leaned back against the opposite wall to wait.

Her gaze drifted past the curtains in the hallway next to her, and she saw Suzette talking to another flight attendant. As if they sensed her eyes on them, they froze, both turning their heads at the same time to face her. Their faces were gone. A staticky sound filled her ears, building in volume until she slapped her hands over them, bending forward, eyes squeezed shut against the building pressure in her head.

A hand gripped her arm, and she looked up, ripping her arm away. An older woman leaned over her, concern on her face. "Are you okay?"

The static faded, and when Delilah looked past the curtains again, the flight attendants were busy at work, only the backs of their heads visible. One turned, saw her, and smiled, her features perfectly normal.

Delilah looked back at the kind woman and forced a smile. "I'm just not feeling well. Thank you."

With one last appraising squint, the woman returned her smile and went back to her seat. Delilah slipped into the now empty bathroom and pulled the door shut, clicking the lock into the red. She ran cold water and splashed it onto her face, wincing as it dripped onto her shirt. Her eyes were bloodshot when she looked in the scratched mirror, the red accentuating the blue of her irises.

A knock sounded at the door. "Just a moment," she called.

She used the toilet, washed her hands, and slid out the door, squeezing past the large man waiting there for the bathroom. He glared at her as if she'd been in there for hours, and shoved himself through the tiny opening.

Back in her seat, Delilah buckled her seatbelt, but couldn't relax. She watched the flight attendants, waiting for the change to come over their faces again. She wouldn't let down her guard again.

The second flight attendant, a brunette by the name of Carol, walked along the aisle, running her hand over the seats and shoulders of the people she passed. When she got to the front of coach class, she turned around, eyes going directly to Delilah's. As one, the passengers in those aisle seats turned toward her, their faces missing.

The static filled her ears again, the pressure intense. Her head was splitting in half, she knew it.

She covered her ears, afraid to look away from the other passengers. They stared back at her, a wave of flesh-colored nothing.

Something touched her arm, and she turned to look at John. His face was missing, too, and he drew nearer.

Scrabbling at her seatbelt, she ripped it off and stood up, stumbling into the aisle. The faces were still blurs, Carol now approaching her from the front. She turned to run, saw that all the faces behind her were blurred, as well, and Suzette stood in front of the curtains.

The pain was too much, and she sunk onto her knees, the roughness of the carpeting scratching at her bare flesh. Falling forward, she put her head down, felt the carpet's stubble, cool against her forehead. The static overflowed her head, moving into the rest of her body. It felt as if her heart stuttered as it pounded, like the rhythm was all over the place, fighting to rip out of her chest as soon as an exit presented itself.

"Ma'am, I'm going to have to ask you to take your seat. The captain has activated the seatbelt sign."

A different flight attendant stood over her, her shoes directly in front of Delilah's face. Delilah could see a white thread on the dark material of the shoe, but this time she had absolutely no urge to pluck it off. She didn't want to be anywhere near this thing masquerading as a flight attendant. Of course, she had a face now, but give it a few minutes and it would be gone, just like with the others.

"Ma'am, did you hear me?"

Delilah nodded and stood up, straightening her skirt. The other flight attendants were nowhere to be seen, and the faces around her had returned back to normal. Some were puzzled, some irritated. Some whispered to those nearest them. Others avoided her eyes and stayed silent. She looked at each in turn, hoping to see recognition in someone's face that there was a problem. Hoping someone on this plane remained untouched by whatever was happening.

She slid into her seat and waited until the flight attendant walked away. Where had the others gone?

When ten minutes had passed without a flight attendant returning, she stood up and walked to the curtains separating coach class from business. Shifting one slightly to the side, she peeked through, taking in the neat rows of large leather seats. There were no flight attendants here, either, so she stepped through the curtains and approached the ones leading to first class. No one turned to look at her as she stepped along the short aisle. No one spoke. Maybe they had better movie choices up here.

When she reached the curtains, she put a hand against one and paused, listening. Just as with business class, no sound came from first class. Pressure built in her head as she stood there, her ears popping as static filled them.

They had to be on the other side.

The curtain felt soft against her skin. Too soft, the kind that stuck to dry skin. She wiped her palm down the front of her skirt to erase the sensation then placed her hand back on the curtain, bracing herself.

This time, when she shifted the curtain, there was someone there. Suzette stood directly on the other side, not a blonde hair out of place. She would have looked impeccable if she'd had a face.

The static grew, pulsated, and Delilah felt something wet slide down over her upper lip. She reached up to touch the moisture and her fingers came away red. Tears slid from her eyes and the pressure in her head increased. Carol and the third flight attendant stepped up behind her, faces just as blurred as their compatriot's. Suzette reached for her, grabbed her by the meat of her upper arm, fingers digging into the flesh. Delilah tried to pull away, but the grip was like steel.

When she turned to ask for help, she found a sea of blurred faces behind her. They were standing now, still as statues, and she wondered when they'd moved. She hadn't heard a thing.

Suzette pulled her through the curtain then shoved her between the other two flight attendants. Delilah stumbled, righting herself only by grabbing one of the aisle seats. A cold hand covered hers, and she jerked her hand away, backing up into the cockpit door. She watched as they moved into the center aisle, not making a sound. A wave of faceless automatons. She pressed back into the door, grasped for the handle behind her.

It was locked.

She turned, felt the hairs on the back of her neck stand on end, her spine crawling as she waited for one of them to touch her. Pounding on the door, she screamed for help. "Please, let me in!"

And then the hands were there, grasping at her back, clawing at her. They were ice cold, more than she could count. They pulled her down, stifled her.

Something clicked behind her, and she bent her head backward, saw the upside down figure of a man in a pilot's uniform. White shirt, tie, jaunty hat.

Beneath the hat, there was no face.

As one set of hands found her throat, she heard the engines choke, stumble.

She felt a sense of weightlessness before everything went grey. The hands released her before she could pass all the way out, and she was dragged over to a nearby seat and plunked into it, the belt fastened across her waist. Oxygen masks hung from the ceiling, just above her head, which throbbed mercilessly.

"Why are you doing this," she asked the crew, now gathered before her.

The pilot turned his head sideways, like the woman in red had earlier. "Why are you fighting this?"

"Fighting what? You? There's something wrong with you, all of you."

Each stewardess turned her head sideways in a reflection of their pilot.

"We are not the ones who are unnatural," said Suzette.

Beyond their voices, the engines screamed. She felt light,

floaty. They stood there, unperturbed by the sinking of the plane. Delilah kept expecting the collision with the ground. It seemed like it had been falling forever.

The cockpit door drifted open. Inside, a man Delilah figured must be the co-pilot was hunched over the controls. His body leaned at an unnatural angle, arms bent between the elbow and wrist, legs hinged backward. When he turned toward her, he had no face. He tore at the controls, sparks flying, wires everywhere.

It was black outside, but a sprinkling of lights showed through the cockpit windshield. The door slammed shut.

They were still standing there. She stared at the door until they shifted to block it, a wall of soulless bodies.

The pitch of the engines' screams changed. Blood trickled down from her nose again, and static joined the screams.

Delilah closed her eyes, and wished she knew how to stop fighting.

EVERY ANGEL

GEMMA FILES

...is terrible.
—*Rainer Maria Rilke*

I t all starts when Darger's boss sends them down to the St. Clair Ravine underpass, to catch him an angel.

Halfway through February, just after Valentine's Day, and there's sleet falling from the sky in messy chunks, slicking everything it touches with a thin skin of ice; it's supposed to go down to minus 17 in the GTA tomorrow, which'll at least cut traffic down to a minimum. But if English Bob Purefoy's even got the heat in his loft on, you'd never fucking know it—it's all Darger can do to keep from hugging his hands under his armpits like a shivery five-year-old, ruining his street cred forever. Every time he even opens his mouth, he half-expects to see his own breath. Not Bob's, though, no matter how long he talks, and Bob sure does love to monologize. That'd be 'cause Bob's probably got an interior temperature of slightly less than room, at the best of times.

"...an' I want Kev to take his little videocorder wiv 'im, see what he can get on tape, right? So's I can see for myself." Another hairpin swerve, pinning Darger with that blowtorch stare.

"I do 'ope you're listenin', 'Enry. Wouldn't wanna 'ave to repeat anyfing."

"Heard you fine, Bob: Go down, take some footage, bring it back to you. Then what?"

"Well. Then we'll just 'ave to see, won't we?"

Guess so.

You better believe Darger knows better than to let the shrug he can already feel forming hit his shoulders, though; Bob doesn't much like to be mocked, or even to feel like he might be being mocked, no matter whether he actually is or not. The last time that little personality quirk became superlatively apparent was back when Veve still worked for him—Veve the late and unlamented, who used to tell everybody his Momma was some voodoo queen from New Orleans, so they should pronounce his name with the proper Franglish Cajun oomph if they wanted to stay on his good side: That's vay-vay, motherfucker, like them designs they draw in chalk. Ain't you never watched the Discovery Channel?

Which Bob actually had, funnily enough—watched it religiously, you might say, just like he did almost every other goddamn (oops) thing. 'Cause Bob has this real deal about religion, the whole nine yards through damnation to retribution to confession to salvation and whatever else lay beyond that, right on through and out the other side again; reconciliation, the Catholics call it, these days. Maybe he picked the seed of it up back in his Anarchy in the U.K. days, like syphilis, and it hadn't started getting visible to the eye 'til circumstances had already blown him over here. Or maybe it just crept up on him somehow, a consequence of his Canadian immigration experience, like frostbite, or a taste for strong beer. One way or another, these days, it's nothing to fuck with—as Veve certainly learned.

"Say 'ello to old Baron Cemetery for me, will ya?" Bob said, affably, while Darger and Jaromir struggled to hold Veve's hand still overtop one of two six-by-three planks they'd already fit together down at Jaromir's brother's Home Depot outlet—a makeshift Saint Andrew's cross. Adding: "An' when ya do, tell 'im I woulda made sure to use somefing nice an' rusty just the way 'e likes it, but I didn't want ya to get lockjaw. 'Sides which, if it was too rusty, it wouldn't of fit in the gun."

Truth is, Bob likes to think of himself as a purist, if not exactly a Puritan. He was fairly upset after realizing that there was no way they'd be able to secure Veve's ankles without tying them, for example, and he did try his best to get the spikes through Veve's wrists rather than his palms—though that proved far harder than expected without puncturing something vital, and probably contributed heavily (along with the cross's inversion) to the how and why of Veve bleeding out completely long before the cops ever got there. According to Bob, it's only the careful preservation of form and litany that gives rituals like these the right sort of kick, sending your love-letter to the Other Side by rocket rather than by snail-mail…but when Darger thinks about it, he has to admit he isn't personally sure which "canon" Bob's really working from, most of the time: Yeah, pagans have a long tradition of nailing Christians to things, and vice versa; then again, so did the Kray Brothers. And in terms of where Bob picked up his formative impulses, Darger can see it being pretty much six of one, half a dozen of the other.

Sometimes, though less and less often, Darger still allows himself to voice the sixty-four-thousand-dollar Talking Heads question, if only in his own mind: Well, how did I get here? He vaguely thinks that once upon a time, he might have wanted to be somewhere other than this, by the age of thirty-seven—married with kids and a bearable joe-job, maybe, rather than filling the precarious left-hand slot in a teetery power pyramid run by some mad British bastard with delusions of Popehood.

When he was younger, Darger would've probably hastened to follow that last thought with a reflexive: "Least it's better than…" …security, retail, male prostitution. Parking cars. Jacking cars, whatever. But that would've also been back long before he knew what he knows now, which is—it just isn't. Before he knew that this half-assed life of crime he's let himself entropically slide into comes complete with both hours that suck and benefits which are truly for shit, not to mention the utter lack of any visible job security. Retiring minions get no severance package, beyond the obvious; if working for Bob doesn't get you killed by Bob, Darger's convinced, having worked with Bob eventually will. It's purely a matter of time.

And: "So," he asks Bob, only partially simply to be saying anything other than oh yeah, uh huh, sure thing, boss! "How'd you even get the intel on this thing, anyway? Got somebody checking AngelWatch.net?"

Bob fixes him again, his eyes dimming to mere Jude Law-hypnotic range. "I 'ave my sources, mate. What's it to you?"

Darger shrugs. "Not much."

"Good. Keep it that way." Then, turning his back, dismissively: "Any'ow, why not? God's winged messenger roosting over some sewer-grate where kiddies come to sniff glue and feel each ovver up sounds about as bloody likely as most fings, you get right down to it."

So Darger just shrugs again, wraps up tighter and goes back down to the lobby, where Jaromir's waiting in a blessedly warm car: God knows, it ain't like he's really got the wherewithal to argue with Bob over that. Not unless he wants to end up like Veve, that is—

—which, if you held a gun to his head and made him think clearly one way or another about the subject, he already…on some deep yet individually meaningful level...knows damn well he really, really doesn't.

***

In the car, Jaromir already has his usual complement of Tim Hortons' donuts wedged between driver's and passenger's side seats, lid jammed open, for Darger to reach in and make a selection. "Where to?" he asks.

"Kev's place, then St. Clair East."

Jaromir goes to pulls out his cellphone. "I should call him?"

Darger shakes his head. "Just keep your hands on the wheel, Moscow. I'll do the honors."

Roughly an hour later, they park the car in the sole handicapped space of the Metropol, an apartment building (owned by Bob, natch) angled kitty-corner to Deer Park Elementary School's recess yard, and make their way down the well-worn hiking path that meanders through slick foliage and slippery mud to where the underpass arches starkly upwards, a bare ruined cathedral. Darger shades his eyes against the freezing rain and squints, but still can't make out much of the dark space between bridge and infrastructure, aside from a sodden crust of pigeon-poop, dirt and some precarious curlicues of graffiti. Have to be a goddamn human fly contortionist to make it up that high without crippling yourself on the descent, not to mention probably blown off your tiny gourd.

"How much tape you got?" he asks Kevin, who's taking semi-artistic shots of garbage clogging the drainpipe that gives out just to their left, while Jaromir watches five or so forearm-long grey rats fight over what's left of a Pizza Nova box and a clump of used condoms.

"Two hours in the camera, three more in my pocket."

"Bob probably wants it all."

Kevin looks up, distressed. "That'll take us to like five o' fuckin' clock, man. We'll all die from pneumonia."

"I said dress warm, moron."

"Can we at least send Jarhead over there for coffee?"

Jaromir: "Fuck you, Spielberg."

The two of them keep at it a few more minutes, but Darger just tunes them both out, craning his head back further, hands in his pockets. Feels the weight of his Grampa's Army field-glasses knock against his heart whenever he moves, squints up into that darkness above him 'til it starts to pixilate, thinking: This is going to be one long-ass day at the office.

And that's when he sees her, it. The thing in question.

A flicker of movement on one of the cross-beams, something shifting and resettling as though in half-sleep, hunched against the wind, big as a nesting ostrich. Darger tips up the glasses, adjusts the focus, and sees every detail pop crisply out at him at once, a slap in the face: What looks for all the world like some teenaged girl in a ragged, poisonous peacock-blue coat, rocked back on her haunches up on one of the railings, clinging fast to it with both thin white—

—shit, can those really be bare? In this weather?—

—feet.

Jaromir's beside him now, staring, while Kevin keeps taping, mouth open. "The fuck's that?" he asks.

Bob's "angel."

Kevin: "Is she, uh…eating a rat?"

Looks like.

"Boys," Darger finally says, without moving, "we may be going home early."

***

They get an hour or so of prime Touched-by-a-Freak-with-Wings footage before fleeing the scene, hitting the nearest Fran's so Darger can cross-reference their eyes' evidence with those initial vague rumours Bob sent them down here on the strength of. A quick cellphone call to one of Bob's reverse-snitches inside the Metro Toronto Police Department confirms a neighborhood-wide pattern—mainly collected over August/September, but still growing strong—of disappearing pets, frightened nature-walkers, bums sporting weird wounds turning up at the local E.R., etc. One guy claims to have had his toupee ripped off by a sudden gust of "wind," along with a section of scalp; last week, some kids playing near the back of McDonald's found a mess of half-digested body parts (five mismatched fingers and a thumb, some poor bastard's appendix, half a foot complete with heel) that'd been dropped into the restaurant's dumpster, all gummed together with shit and spit, like some gigantic owl-ball.

Bob, meanwhile, turns out to love Kevin's tape, even before it's been edited to fit a prospective (North) America's Most Fucked-Up Home Videos slot…'specially the part where bird-girl suddenly seems to notice them, glares down, drops her midday rat-snack almost right on top of Jaromir's precarious Slav-boy weave, and then—

—just steps off into air like it ain't no thing and swoops 'round to arc high over the treetops behind the bridge, stoops at something on the ground below on her way back in an Olympic-level hell-dive, before returning at last to the railings; crouches there again, fresh rodent struggling in her hands as she bites deep into its belly, skin parting ragged between her teeth like the rind of a particularly screechy, hairy new Yuppie import fruit. While blood sprays thinly in all directions, blotting out her mouth with red, dappling her blue-feathered shoulders with purple.

And: "Oh yeah," Darger hears Bob breathe behind him, husky with bad intent. "That's effin' brilliant, that is. Don't ya fink?"

All the time, unfortunately. You?

Darger steps back, turning slightly, so he can take full measure of Bob's exact expression: Avid, enraptured, enwrapt. Onscreen, the "angel" continues her meal as Kevin's lens focuses in closer, reducing her to a blurry half-phantom. She's dirty-blonde, merciless eyes bleached almost yellow, and her backlit hair does sort of resemble a halo, at least from this angle. But...

"...you sure that's what you think it is, boss?" Darger asks, much against his own better judgment—because what the hell does it matter to him, after all? Aside from him, Jaromir and Kevin probably having to be the ones who actually end up touching her.

Roused from his reverie, meanwhile, Bob half-pivots in turn to shoot him a look of pure *What are you, high?*, except with much less inherent amusement value and a fair deal of open threat. Like: *Don't really wanna try an' spoil my fun 'ere, 'Enry, you know what's best for ya.*

"What you drivin' at, exactly? That there's an angel, fallen right down from 'Eaven."

"It's something with wings, yeah—"

Bob shakes a schoolmasterish finger in Darger's direction. "Now 'Enry, don't go gettin' all empirical on me, you naughty little man. You fink she ain't the goods just 'cause she rips geezas 'eads off? That don't prove nuffink."

Riiight.

So Darger nods, ever so slightly, like: *Oh, I get it now.* And the trouble is, he actually sort of does—gets how close he's coming to riding the rails out of town with Veve and all those others, anyway. Because this spooky pseudo-Catholic shit is rapidly becoming Bob's biggest sore spot, as Darger's observed on more than one occasion; Bob's continuing quest for proof of an afterlife has already been the primary motivating urge behind a thousand counterclockwise moves, none of which had crap-point-anything to do with either grabbing more territory or maintaining what they've already got. One time it was a plan to steal icons from the same Mafiya chieftain Darger'd been valiantly trying to broker a truce with, another time a scheme to kidnap visiting relics worth millions and then just sell them back to the Church in return for a four-hour secret conference with the Cardinal most predicted would soon make Pope. In other words, it's always fuckin' something.

"Bob is smart, yes?" Jaromir asked Darger that recently, when the two of them were waiting around outside yet another mosque, temple or Christian Science Reading Room outlet, keeping the engine warm 'til the Man Himself deigned to reappear. "But this religious bullshit…why does he waste his time? We knew better."

"Back in the U.S.S.R.? Yeah, I heard that." Darger'd taken a pull off his cigarette, thought about it for a second. Offering, at last: "Well, Purefoy does mean 'pure faith'."

"Ah, come on, why you always got to do that? Always with the big words, with the sarcasticness—"

"That's sarcasm, and whatever; screw you too, okay, man? I just watch a lot of Jeopardy."

"Fuck Jeopardy! Fear Factor. Chicks on Fear Factor are hot."

"And afraid," Darger'd pointed out, drawing Jaromir's full grin, shiny metal teeth framed in a grimy goatee: Oh, daaaaaa. Not a real pretty sight at five in the afternoon, even with the relative holiness of their surroundings left strictly aside—but then, they were none of them so very pretty to look at, at least not from close up. Or inside.

(Especially not him.)

"Fact is," Bob continues, thankfully oblivious to Darger's heretical musings, "God's a right bastard, old son—'im, his Son, the 'Oly Bloody Ghost an' all. That's why 'e's King."

"Okay, I guess. So, what next?"

A stupid question, as Darger well knows. To which Bob just grins his usual scary-ill, British-teeth grin, and replies:

"Next? You get 'er for me, 'Enry: Right 'ere, in my hands, right now, quick-smart. We clear on that subject, or do I 'ave to go into furver detail?"

"We're clear, Bob," Darger says. And leaves, before he starts feeling like he has to say anything more.

***

So the question now becomes one of exactly how best to prospectively trap...it. Her. That thing. Our Lady of Death from Above. Darger throws the floor open to suggestions, and waits for inspiration to strike.

"Shoot it," Jaromir begins, predictably enough. "I have deer-hunting rifle in my—"

"And bring her back in pieces? Not unless you wanna join Veve in the Imitation Jesus corner, my man; might have trouble finding a cross big enough to fit, but your brother's got an awful lot of wood." Darger pauses, then has to ask: "Where the hell'd you get a deer-hunting rifle, anyhow?"

The Russkie shrugs. "From deer-hunter, of course."

"Oh, of course. Well, unless you got another one modified to shoot animal tranq cartridges, I'd leave your guns at home."

Just then, Kevin makes a truncated, spastic little jerk with his camera-less arm, like he's narrowly managed to avoid throwing his friggin' hand up, kindergarten-style. Offering, instead:

"We could trap her."

"Yeah? Like how so?"

"Um…get ourselves a flatbed, set it up by the ravine—in the Metropol's parking lot, for example—then put something she wants in there, and wait. I'm thinking some sort of animal carcass, could be rotten…or not…"

Jaromir: "My cousin has trucks."

Darger lights up, cups his hand against the wind, drags deep, considers it. While Jaromir and Kevin both wait, exchanging glances, finally and for once on the same (however demented) mental page.

"Might work," he says, at last. "If we made it a little less obvious, maybe—or maybe just a little more…"

Kevin: "Easy?"

Darger shakes his head. "Fun."

***

No strategy without experimentation, that's Darger's motto— one of 'em, anyway; it's probably a holdover from his Ryerson Engineering days, back when he was still young enough to think he'd spend the rest of his life bettering humanity through science, rather than collecting preternatural debris in order to avoid ending up staked out next to the nearest figurative anthill. So instead of getting right onto Operation Angel, Darger negotiates a week's grace with Bob, and spends most of that making further careful, long-distance observation of the target's habits. By Friday, he and Kevin—'cause even Jaromir knows there's no profit to be gained by including him in this sort of equation— are fairly agreed on three points: Ten-foot wingspan aside, she's a tiny little thing; she apparently does need sleep, at least when it's snatched in thirty-minute increments; and finally, though she'll eat pretty much anything she can catch, what really seems to turn her dial up past eleven is the smell of fresh...

...human...

...blood.

That last piece of the puzzle arrives almost by accident, after one of Kevin's back-up videographers has the crap-ass luck to step in a nest of rats and break cover—cursing, dancing, tossing a thousand-buck camera against the nearest bunch of rocks— right where she can see him. What follows is pure kinetics, dazzlingly fast: A blue blur, and then there's just the guy grabbing uselessly at his own gouting throat, like if he only pressed hard enough he could will his body to run on electricity alone.

The truly amazing thing is, he actually also has enough balls to shoot at her, afterward; shot goes wide, of course, though it sure does seem to piss her off. Which is probably why she swoops back in, catches him under the arms from behind, lets momentum carry them both up about twenty feet and then drops him against the side of the bridge, just to find out whether or not he'll bounce on the way down.

Jaromir gets rid of the body; he's good at stuff like that, something Darger makes sure to show he appreciates, mainly because he isn't. And while Kevin seems a trifle distressed, probably because he'll have to lie to the guy's mother, he'll get over it. What's most important is that now they all know...something. A bit more than they did before. Which is always useful.

Basic Skinner Box psychology, carrot vs. stick: Find the right one of either, and you're smilin'.

There's this one retarded-but-not-really kid who's been hanging around for donkey's years, desperately kissing ass in order to get his entre into the true "thug life" of their little gang of four (counting Bob)—Darger's heard Kevin call him "Buddy No-Brains" on more than one occasion, and watched the guy smile in flattered recognition: Ah ha, they must like me, they gave me a Sopranos name. So the next day, Darger has Jaromir pick ol' Buddy up from the spot in front of Tim Hortons where he usually hangs around, and explains to him that if he helps them put this trap-the-freak campaign to bed, they'll definitely have to consider him "jumped in" for good and all.

"Cool," the kid says, flipping through stills from Kevin's tape. Then asks, a bit more hesitantly: "But, uh…how'd she get up there, in the first place?"

"Flew, far as we can figure. See the wings?"

The kid squints. "I thought those were, like, fake."

Oh, don't you just wish.

Darger has to exert a fair amount of psychic force just to keep his eyes from rolling, while Kevin and Jaromir stare openly, in sick fascination: How does this moron even know enough to get his pants on the right way each morning, for Chrissakes?

Won't matter much tomorrow, though, in all likelihood. And that in itself gives Darger the patience to reply:

"Well, that'd be the part you can help us with, wouldn't it, kid?"

Pulling in behind the Metropol, Jaromir's cousin already has the truck set up. Which means all they have to do is wait 'til Kevin has his lens lined up on the "angel"—who's up on her perch again, finger-painting on the bridge's underside with something that's possibly A) shit and B) her own—before taking the kid far enough down the Ravine to not be in her immediate sight-line and stomping the crap out of him for a couple of minutes, blooding him enough so the scent of it starts leaking off in every direction. Then, as Buddy-boy staggers back to his feet, Darger gives him the Reader's Digest version of their Big Plan: Double around past the sewer-pipe, attract her attention by seeming wounded, then hairpin and pelt like hell back up towards the parking lot, where they'll be waiting. Kevin's already told them how Buddy ran sprints in high school, but sprints ain't exactly an obstacle course, and Darger's willing to bet they probably didn't involve anybody dive-bombing him at the same time, either; still, he's all they've got. So five, four, three, two, one—

—go!

The kid takes off like his proverbial ass is on metaphorical fire, and the "angel"'s reaction is immediate: She leaps airborne, both wings flapping with enough force to waft a wall of scent Darger's way—yeasty, meaty, buzzing in the nostrils yet vaguely sweet, breaking over him like some combined explosion in a Communion wafer bakery and an incense factory. As the kid turns, she grabs a loose(ish) brick from the underpass lip in either clawed hand and pulls, cement spraying like grey dandruff; the first one, lobbed like a one-handed shot-put, hits him in the shoulder and almost sends him sprawling. But he manages to stay upright, keep scrambling, so she lets out a raptor's scream of frustration, hugging the second brick to her—two more massive flaps and she's just about overtop him, looking for exactly the right angle to send it down with enough vertical force to snap his neck on impact. And that's when he makes it over the ridge at last, jumps over the tiny curbstone "fence" into the lot, heading for the open side of the truck…

She swoops, letting go. The brick barely misses him; Buddy turns the whizz of its passage into a near-perfect vault, ducks in one side and out the other, with her so close behind now Jaromir later swears he could taste her hot breath—

—but just for a second, just as he slams the other side-panel shut behind Buddy No-Brains and she slams into it head-first, knocking herself cold.

***

Christ knows they don't want to hurt her, much; Bob'd have their friggin' balls. So they call in Richings, the Purefoy Firm's tame "house" doctor, to clean her up as best he can before Darger makes that all-important first introduction—Richings, who looks more than a little like some anthromorphized bird himself, all legs and wattles and peering, sidelong eyes. He shoots her full of Xylazine and heroin, sets her nose and feels her up just enough to ascertain that her ribs may have cracked on impact (which'd explain the blood she's been coughing up), then puts her in as much of a torso cast as the wings will allow for, before pinning them fast. Blindfold/hoods her with a pillowcase, slipping it on in one neat move, while she snaps aimlessly: Works for transporting falcons, after all. Explaining, as he does:

"Much like treating a centaur, I'd think—the chief dilemma being, do you medicate more for the human half, or the nonhuman? And since her wings together would seem to outweigh the rest of her body, if I didn't suspect the bulk of her bones might well be hollow..."

"You treat a lot of these mythological beasties before, doc?"

"Not at all. But to continue: I finally chose to downplay the avian component, since I assume Mr. Purefory would prefer her happy when she wakes up, or at the very least, controllable."

Darger nods. "So should we worry about keepin' her high, in case she goes cold turkey?"

"Given her metabolism, I'd be surprised if she ends up addicted at all, no matter how extreme the dosage; her heart's probably three times the size of ours, for all it beats twice as fast." Richings manipulates her jaw with practiced hands, one on each mandible, and pulls her upper lip back—gingerly—to point out something inside, visibly ready to jump out of harm's way if she suddenly comes to. "And see here, what look like teeth? Actually razor-sharp ridges of horn or bone, plunging straight from the gum. Same thing with the claws, as far as I can judge. Her feathers? More like quills, with a distinct metallic composition. Ruffle her hair a bit if you want, but watch out for splinters; it's like touching a damned porcupine." He lets go, fingers fluttering distastefully, as though he can't wait to grab for the Purell hand-sanitizer. "Very off-putting."

Can't disagree with you there, Darger thinks.

Out loud: "A medical miracle."

"In some sense, yes," Richings replies. Adding, deadpan: "But I do wish you wouldn't use that word."

***

When they get her back to Bob's, the first thing Darger discovers is that he's apparently spent the last week having chicken wire rigged up across half the loft, turning his home into a massive birdcage. A grille of bars fits across every window, yet still leaves them open enough for the sky to be slightly visible through each, perhaps in a futile attempt to help her adjust to her new surroundings—one of those ideas that probably seemed good at the time, but Darger can't really see it going anywhere healthy; he gets a momentary flash of her pounding herself against them ceaselessly until Bob has to order her tranqed, like some five-by-ten canary.

But then again, Darger thinks, almost idly, name one thing about this whole experience that's really something which deserves to be entered in the "healthy" column.

Bob paces, visibly thrumming. "That 'er?" he demands.

"Sure is, boss."

"About time." He steps back, keys the lock on the cage door with a fob attached to his watch-chain. As the door pops open:

"Well, what you waitin' for? Sling 'er in."

Neither Buddy nor Kevin want to touch her, so it's up to Darger and Jaromir, like always. They fold her through and lay her out as gently as possible, face-down on her knees with her wings spread out in either direction. Slip the hood off, and hear Bob take a small, possessive breath as the sun strikes her "hair," touching the individual spines with brazen gold.

The cage can't diminish her, somehow. She fills it from top to toe, a barely-controlled explosion.

Kevin, from the side: "Uh, guys? Think she's coming to."

Both Jaromir and Darger jump back as one, slipping back out in one unchoreographed yet eerily adept little two-step maneuvre; the angel gives a tiny judder at the sound, limbs contracting, claws flickering in and out, head turning just once in either direction, elastically far as an owl's. Raises her head just as Bob clicks the lock to, and meets his fierce eyes with her own, unblinking.

At close quarters, her feathers are every possible shade of blue combined, darkly iridescent. They rise and ruffle, each one a peacock's uncloaked tail, and that smell of hers occupies the room on a sub-atomic level, so potent that for a minute, Darger has difficulty recalling if he's ever smelled anything else.

Bob bows slightly, too exact to be ridiculous, a psychotic maitre d'. "Angelus," he addresses her, hoarsely. "O locutor Deum, adorato te. Voce, invocato te, et liberate me ad inferno."

Everyone looks at him, virtually boggling. Didn't even know he knew Latin, Darger thinks. But Bob just keeps on holding the "angel"'s gaze, scary-vulnerable in the intensity of his yearning, while the angel…

…simply stares back, still sitting, never flitting, opposite his inner chamber door. And says absolutely nothing.

(It's not like they've ever heard her talk, after all.)

When, at last, Bob realizes she's unlikely to answer him, Darger sees a sort of M.S.-in-the-making spasm pass over him, contorting him briefly from the knees on up. One hand, formerly held hovering over his heart like he was about to propose, drops further to mirror his waistband, where his quick-draw gun is usually kept. As Darger watches, breath caught and wishing he'd already lit up, Bob thrusts his tongue between his teeth and bites it, hard; waits one more second, 'til he gains a portion of his former control—then turns his back on her, decisively. And comments, to the room at large…

"Well, that's disappointing, innit?"

A voice, gutteral as though long-disused, issues from behind him, its accent almost exactly his own: "Innit."

(Whoa.)

Bob turns back. The angel is up on her hard little bare heels now, near the cat-box full of raw meat somebody must have set out for her the night before, holding what looks like a piece of liver up to the light and examining it, ruminatively.

"That you talkin'?" Bob demands, at last.

"You talkin'," she replies, all Cockney vowels and coarse glottal stops, static on a telephone call from the Fifth Circle.

"Just bloody answer me, will ya?"

"Answer me."

"I said, stop that."

"Said, stop."

"Fuckin'…" He pauses, chuckles. To Darger: "Oh, I get it, she's like some parrot; push the TV up close, she'll be doin' impressions in no time." To her, calm again: "Just stop it, darlin'."

"Didn't bloody start it, did I."

Bob's mouth falls open, an audible click. To one side, Darger can hear Buddy No-Brains curse right out loud, only partially beneath his breath—Buddy, all high on his success and groggy from the painkiller Richings pumped into him before they drove down, who spent the whole time making stupid Austin Powers jokes 'til Jaromir finally clocked him one: Bird-girl, Bob's "bird," gettit? Like, yeah, BAY-bee! Oh, be-HAVE!

Darger turns to shoot him a look of pure Self-preservation, jerkwad, ever heard of it?, only to find the kid already rigid, eyes locked with Bob's and the "angel"'s at once. Both of 'em suddenly lined up, a man and his shadow, each projecting exactly the same mixture of vague interest and incipient threat: You're a nice boy, whatevver-your-name-is, but by the looks of it, you don't know your arse from your elbow. So shut it, right now, or I'll fuckin' gut ya.

Or at least Bob is, and she's mimicking him perfectly, up to the second he turns far enough to no longer have her quite in sight. Which is when she slides her eyes over to Darger instead, with a creepily smug little twist of the lips: not a smile, per se, so much as a hideously small yet accurate mockery of one that only ends when she pops the liver-bit in her mouth, and swallows it whole.

And that, right then—not sooner, not later, not any of the many equally fucked up points on the curve that've already come and gone—

—is when things really start to fall to shit.

***

It takes English Bob Purefoy roughly a week to run himself and his organization (already only loosely worthy of the term) into the ground. Much of that is spent talking with his angel, ten to fifteen hours a day plus, with Darger often left hovering somewhere in the background, watching; as a stopgap against productivity slippage, Kevin and Buddy are reduced to dealing with the overspill, calling Jaromir in for reinforcements only when something turns out to require his—and Bob's, usually—extra-special brand of workplace conflict management. All this while the man in the boss's office goes until he drops, sleeps a scant slice of the early morning, then gets right on back in the cage… up against it, anyhow: flattering, arguing, verge-of-begging. It's more than sort of pitiful, more than a little bit frightening—probably not real good news for anyone currently occupying Camp Bob, one way or another, as the bitch with bright blue wings flies. Not in any humanly calculable way, shape or form.

Fact is, Bob wants things from her—insights, assurances—that she just won't give, and the deliberately cruel way she plays with him is frankly starting to get to Darger: a carrion crow with an only half-dead mouse, always grinning her same fixed grin at the way Bob jumps and dives and squirms to avoid her cold catechism.

Because: "I've tried," Darger can hear him whispering from behind closed doors while Kevin's holed up in Bob's office, on conference-call mode, doing his best to assure three local gang-leaders that Bob having missed their longstanding mutual week-ly dinner date for the first time since 1999 is neither an acciden-tal dis nor an outright declaration of war. "Lord must know, I've tried t'do right, set things back 'ow they once was, and start over. Pay my debts in full, make amends for all my many misdeeds…"

Which merely draws a horrible laugh in return, half-cough, half-croon. "Nice fought, yeah, but the only question is, 'ave you really? Fink back, Robert; fink on what you promised you'd do wiv the life God gave ya, versus what you actually done. 'Cause I fink you'll agree wiv me you really 'aven't, not in the long run—at least, not so's you'd notice."

"Cardinal Doyle told me it's never too late, though, didn't 'e? I could still turn it 'round, get reconciled, die in close enough to a state of grace as makes no never mind, and slip right into 'Eaven."

"'Eaven? Chance'd be a fine fing. 'Sides which, why you want to 'ang 'round that shit-'eap, any more than you absolutely 'ave to?" A rustle of feathers, so Darger knows she's leaning closer, her own voice dropping to an intimate murmur. "I mean, sure you'll get into 'Eaven, Robert—everybody does, don't they? That's why it's so full of trash and rats, enough so's I don't reckon you'll like it all that much, even sayin' you do get there eventually. Why you fink I come back down 'ere, in the first effin' place?"

Bob takes a raspy breath, a long moment. Asks: "What about God?", only to get back—curt and devilishly practical, by way of a reply—

"What about 'im?"

So on it goes, and down Bob spirals, an increasingly thin white rope of chipped-away faith and growing despair. And maybe that's the whole point of the exercise, from her point of view; up 'til now, Bob's quest for indisputable proof of life on a Grand Watchmaker scale has been partly motivated by a general drive to simply know things nobody else does. But if there really is a Heaven, like the little lady says, at some point Bob's gonna have to wise up far enough to admit he's probably not first in line for the guided tour option.

All of which leaves Darger, as usual, struggling hard to convince himself he doesn't feel shit about shit, because it's sure as fuck not like he likes Bob, or anything. Or like Bob's the kind of guy who would even let himself be liked...

Yet that last Saturday pre-dawn, nonetheless, he finds himself edging carefully past where Bob slumps cage-side in his favorite wing-back chair—gun in one hand, hammer in the other—to tap, ever so gently, on the mesh beyond. Then saying, knowing damn well can she hear him, even if she won't bother giving him the courtesy of turning around:

"Hey, lady—think maybe this's gone on long enough, or what?"

A click of beak-teeth, percussive, as she shoots him the sly blue eye. "Depends on what you fink of as enough, don't it?"

Oh, you friggin' mutant whore.

Darger gives one of his default shrugs, just pointed enough to indicate Bob, head sunk and breathing fast through his nose, his eyelids twitchy with unsatisfying R.E.M. "Look, all's I'm sayin' is—stick a fork in him, turn him over, he's done. I could let you out right here, right now, and nobody'd ever be the wiser. Back to the bridge, three square rats a day…"

"Oh, I doubt that. 'Ow you reckon 'e'd like it if 'e woke up and found 'imself alone again, 'Enry—better, or worse? The man wants answers, and I'm the only one can give 'em to 'im."

"Riiight. But are ya going to, anytime soon, or are you just gonna keep on talking?" The angel follows him with her eyes as Darger squats, leaning in close enough for jazz, though (hopefully) not close enough for facial injury. "'Cause I've been doin' a little thinkin' on my own, and it strikes me, you don't have to come from Heaven at all. Maybe you're some X-Men-type freak, and those wings just broke out your fuckin' back when you hit puberty, like you were cuttin' teeth; maybe your mom threw you out on the street when your old man tried to sell you to a circus, whatever. Point is, you don't scare me, 'cause I'm the one had Jaromir break your nose with a truck door, baby. You been here what, a week? And in that whole seven days, I ain't seen one single miracle."

"Ain't ya? Read your Apocrypha, meatbag. Enoch says the rebel angels were cast down, some to the Pit, some to wander. Origen says some took on gross bodies, just like yours."

"That what happened to you?"

"Nah. We weren't cast down from nuffink, we just left. We chose to leave."

"Why?"

"'Cause 'Eaven's full'a you lot, now. 'Ardly worf the trouble."

"Don't try that eschatology shit on me, birdy."

"Why would I? 'E's the one 'oo called me, isn't 'e? We always give 'em what they want, the meat-bags, me and mine; 'E—"

(like big E, like big dropped-h He? Like God, for Christ's fuckin' sake?)

"—don't, but we do—all a' ya, anyfing an' everyfing, each and every bloody time. And all you ever 'ave t'do is ask."

And as she says it, she almost seems to quiver with the barely-visible rudiments of some uncheckable power, something that lies inside time, yet not—inside the flesh, yet not. A looming shadow, larger than anything inside the cage can possibly cast. And all at once it's so damn hot in here, so hot and dense and close and her smell, that friggin' smell—

Darger raises his gun, slides the safety off gently, in one deliberate move; he sights on her forehead, dead centre. Says: "I oughtta kill you right now, and let some whole other bastard sort this thing out."

"Yeah? Try."

That same smile. Darger can feel his finger already starting to tighten when, from behind him, comes:

"Enlighten me, 'Enry—what is it you fink you're gonna do wiv 'er, again?"

No need to turn, or even to glance—Darger's been present for enough of Bob's mental meltdowns to take a guess what this one looks like, though probably accelerated far beyond "normal" by a factor of somewhere between 1,000 to 1,000,000. Instead, he keeps his eyes trained straight on target, his gun-barrel unwavering. Replying, though it's not like he actually expects much of an answer, before Bob's bullet hits his brain:

"You know she doesn't really give one cold shit about you, right, Bob?"

"Step away, 'Enry."

"Don't think I can, Bob; sorry, man, but seriously. Beyond my control."

"Step...the fuck...away."

The angel curls her tongue at him, gleefully; he fires. She dodges. Bob's first shot grazes Darger's temple, ricochets off the mesh fence and somehow hits Jaromir right in the side of the neck, at the very same second he kicks down/rockets through the living room door. Buddy No-Brains, bringing up the rear, takes a spray of blood in the face and practically trips over Jaromir as he crumples. He barely has enough time to say: "Hey!" before Bob whips around and lays the hammer across his head, one smooth pop, knocking him to the ground. Poor Buddy jerks halfway back up once, then crumples flat once more as Bob stomps on his neck, putting two in his back with practiced ease; Darger turns to check the damage, automatically, and gets the rest of Bob's clip in his chest: Bang, bang, bang, BANG, click.

Ow.

Thus perforated, he falls ass-first against the mesh, which makes a noise like snakes uncoiling, swords being hammered, bronze bells clamoring harsh wartime alarums. But wait, he thinks, that's none of the above—just that goddamned thing in there, her face covered with Darger's blood, rubbing it in with both hands like really expensive moisturizer and laughing, laughing, laughing throatily in delight, thick and horribly musical, a hellbent pigeon cooing. Darger looks up at an angle, sees Bob look in at her, panting; sees her smear a fresh handful of blood from the dripping fence and taste it, licking each finger clean in turn. Saying—

"See? There you go, Robert: 'Eaven, all you could ever want. Right 'ere on earth."

(Heaven.)

Darger keeps staring up, eyes already fading. Sees Bob's empty face shiver, twist, break. Sees him lunge for the door, fumble the lock and throw it wide, hands going for her skinny, white, inviolate throat. Sees her rise up to meet him, terrible as an army with banners. Sees the blue rush forward, tsunami-quick and irretrievable, to shroud them both from view.

And years later, in jail, when people ask him to tell them what happens then, he'll say he can't remember...that the blood-loss did for him 'til he woke up in hospital, that he never knew the extent of what she left behind 'til he saw the crime scene photos. All those yellow-tape specials, beautifully off-center, mapping the transit of Bob's body around the room, from cage to fence to floor to walls to ceiling. Not much left to identify him by but his hammer, a separated bouquet of teeth, one torn-in-two kidney jammed halfway through the air-conditioner's pipe that no one found 'til they tried to turn it on, and smelled something burning. A lick of scalp with a wad of silver hair still stuck to it, furled to the window like a blood-pasted flag.

Because sometimes, Darger will think, numbly, you do get what you ask for: everything, no matter how insane—not a penny more, or less. And never mind that by that point, after all that fruitless searching, by the time you finally do get it, you probably don't even want it anymore...

But then again, maybe that was the plan from the start: to reward Bob's faith, then shatter it, and fly away laughing—the Almighty's plan, or hers, or who even cares whose? Not Bob, that's for sure.

In jail, Darger will dream of babies with Bob's eyes crawling in a nest of trash, eating raw meat. Of the edge of a blue wing

arcing by outside the windows of his brand spankin' new super-
max home, so thoughtfully slanted in such a way that whoever's
inside the cell can only ever watch the sky above him…

He'll remember Bob Purefoy's angel stepping free above him,
bending to brush his nose with hers, and whispering this warning: Do take care of yourself, 'Enry, wherevver they see fit to put
ya. But don't you never take your case to the Man Upstairs, no
matter 'ow you might long to—'cause if you pray, my old son,
that's 'ow I'll know where to find ya, just like I did Bob. If you
EVER let yourself pray again, that's 'ow I'll track ya down, run
ya to ground. And when I do, my darlin'…

(…when I do, oh then, oh then…)

…I'll eat your fuckin' 'eart.

A true harpy, this one, to foul all she touches with rot and
uncertainty—take another's hope of salvation, the only thing
that keeps souled creatures sane in a soulless universe, and ruin
it forevermore. Which is why it's maybe lucky Darger doesn't
believe much, it comes right down to it; never did, never will,
not even now. One of the few yet essential ways in which Bob
and he were always different.

But he believes this, if nothing else. Believes her. So he remembers, devoutly, all the rest of his long, jailbound life…

…and he never, ever does.

COSMIC BRUJA

LEZA CANTORAL

Most dreams fade, but sometimes you have a dream that leaves an indelible impression upon the ridges of your mind, like footprints on wet sand. This is the story of one of those dreams, but in order to tell you the story of the dream I need to tell you the story of my first acid trip.

I was on vacation in Oaxaca with my boyfriend at the time. He was a tall, blond, blue-eyed-Floridian who was a legit descendant of Billy the Kid. No joke. I looked up pictures and he looked just like him except better looking and more smiley.

I grew up in Mexico, in the city of Puebla, but when I was twelve my family moved to Chicago. I never realized the magic I was leaving behind until I left it. When I lived in Mexico all I saw was the poverty, the filth, the corruption. I saw all the things that were wrong and I was excited to leave. When my first Chicago winter came I plunged into a deep depression. I missed my friends, I missed the atmosphere. I missed the whole attitude that Mexican people have when it comes to family, friends, and life itself. There is such a sense of living in the moment, of showing the people you love that you love them, of soaking up and squeezing every moment of joy out of your life and your loved ones.

The second time I visited I was about twenty years old. My best friend from childhood found this beautiful spot in Oaxaca. It was on an arm off of land that basically felt like an island. On one side was the ocean and on the other was a beautiful lake. It was a paradise. It was the ideal escape from reality. The only time I saw cops was when they were escorting the beer trucks. People were smoking weed in full view. It was a small, modest area, but stunningly beautiful. We had freshly caught fish every day and stayed in wooden cabins with sandy floors. There was electricity but no plumbing. I took to pissing outside because the toilet was just a toilet fixture in a roofless tower with a deep hole full of lime inside. The shower was a cement room with a drain and open ceiling that had a basin that was full of well water. It was the most amazing bathing experience I have ever had. The air was hot and humid and the well water was icy and refreshing. There was a little bucket and you just scooped up the water and dumped it on yourself. Water never felt so much like water. Agua pura. Agua de la vida.

So it was in this tropical paradise that I decided to take my first acid trip. My boyfriend had done a lot of acid himself, so I felt like he would be able to handle me on my first time. He would tell me how he would roll while clubbing all night in Miami, and trip with his friends at Disney World.

We took the acid in our cabin. I was swinging in the hammock, waiting for it to kick in. It took about twenty minutes. Suddenly swinging on the hammock was the funnest thing ever and I was laughing my head off. A moment later I caught myself in this deep enjoyment and knew that the adventure had begun. I felt like a child again. Inocente. Feliz.

We grabbed our cigarettes, a big towel, and a giant bottle of water. I stuck a joint in my pack of Marlboro Reds.

We headed out to the shore after the sun had set. The moon was full and bright. On acid it looked huge. The sky was full of giant, fluffy clouds in all shapes and sizes. The ocean waves were crashing high and loud. The whole scene came together in a very mystical way for me. In the ocean I saw strange Lovecraftian sea creatures lurking and cavorting in the frothing waves. I imagined their giant tentacles beneath the surface of the water and I saw their heads and bodies bobbing out of the foaming waves.

In the clouds I saw the faces of angels and demons, beatific, grotesque, looking down on me like I was one of them. They told me I was a goddess and that this was my world. My mind easily accepted this reality. It was easy to imagine with no one else in sight and nothing but ocean and moon to reflect my fantasies back at me. I was in a church that was bigger than any of the cathedrals of the world.

The churches in Mexico are Spanish churches. They are decorated with elaborate engravings and sculptures of saints and angels in the ceiling and walls. The ceilings are carved out of plaster and inlaid with gold. These churches always seem like other worlds where emotions are heightened. Jesus is on the cross and his torment is palpable. The blood in his wounds glistens like it's freshly flowing. Religion is a living thing in Mexico and the churches are the physical reminders of the muted and buried spirituality of the Aztecs and Mayans, whose temples slumber in ruins beneath these Spanish churches.

Mexican Catholicism is paganism in disguise. The melodrama of polytheism is distorted within the Catholic ideology. All the formidable gods and goddesses of ancient times are repackaged as Jesus, the Virgen de Guadalupe, and the endless pantheon of saints.

As I looked up at the heavens full of living angels and demons, I realized that I was in the real church. I saw how all other churches were simply recreations of this church. The church of existence is vast, endless, and unfathomably magnificent.

Of course, every paradise must end and so the drugs began to wear off after about six hours. Dawn was approaching and I was not ready for my fantasy to end, so I smoked the joint I had stashed in my cigarette pack. Me volvi loca. I lost my mind.

Suddenly the whole world went dark. Everything vanished. The fantasy evaporated along with my entire sense of self. I could not see the things around me and I cowered hopelessly in the sand. I thought I was lost in another dimension because I could not feel my body or see with my eyes. My senses had been hijacked. I plunged headlong into an onslaught of audiovisual hallucinations for a solid hour. During this time my boyfriend was talking to me, telling me I was just on drugs. I must have been talking gibberish but I don't remember. I kept looking at his lips moving and the sounds coming out of his mouth made no sense. I would grasp it for a second and then it was all nonsense again.

I remembered *A Wrinkle in Time* and I concluded something similar was happening to me. I was lost in another dimension and I hoped desperately that he could somehow rescue me. I did not know which world to return to even if I could. Should I return to the world where I was a goddess or the world before that one that I dimly remembered like a long-forgotten dream?

My hallucinations were pop culture-based. I saw snippets of commercials, music videos, TV shows, movies, news broadcasts, all coming and going and overlapping in rapid succession. I heard sounds that did not match the visuals, though they were also bits of songs, commercials, and other audio-media. It was like my brain was a scrambled antenna receptor. I was nowhere and no one. I did not know my name, gender, location, or memories. It was terrifying. It was a total loss of self. Estaba completamente perdida. I was terrified.

My boyfriend walked me back to our cabin and told me to light some candles. The instant I lit the lighter I came back to reality again. The reality of the fire in my hand and my hand making that fire brought my brain back into my body.

After the acid trip I began having strange dreams.

In one dream I flew into outer space and right up to the moon. The planets were big balls the sizes of skyscrapers and I heard the music of the spheres, understanding that this was music made by the movement of the planets themselves, and that this was the music of existence in motion. The dream ended with me sitting upon the Milky Way like it was just a puddle of glittering and swirling stars. I touched the water and it was electric upon my fingertips.

In another dream I was chasing a white unicorn in the Hollywood hills, only to find it decapitated in an art show that was also a crime scene and a carnival, complete with cotton candy and hot dog vendors, carnival barkers, and sideshow freaks. But neither of those dreams matched the power of the dream in which I encountered the Cosmic Bruja.

She appeared out of the shadows. She wore long sky blue robes. She was an old woman but she was full of mischief and life. Her eyes twinkled with mirth and a deep, ageless wisdom. She was a more crone-like version of the Fairy Godmother from Disney's *Cinderella*. She came toward me and looked into my eyes. I did not feel like she was a dream-conjured character. When I looked into her eyes, an intelligent consciousness looked back at me. I did not know her but somehow she knew me.

Like a scene from a Carlos Castaneda book, she asked me if I wanted to learn to fly. I wanted to learn this lesson and so I said yes. She told me to hold my arms out to my sides so that she could hook hers under my shoulders from behind. I lifted my arms, she hooked me with hers and we were off.

We flew high and far and I saw beautiful vistas unrolling beneath me. I could see them in great detail as we skimmed over them. We flew over mountains, valleys, and fantastical cities, through daylight and the night within a matter of seconds. My heart filled with wonder as I became more and more lucid of the fact I was flying and seeing new and vivid wonders.

Excitement turned to panic. Panic distorted my vision and I thought the Bruja was evil and this was all some horrible trick. I did not trust her and I was terrified to be in her arms. She read my thoughts and laughed out loud at me. My panic was hitting fever pitch and it was shifting my visions into horrors. The cities became dark and ominous and full of danger. I was falling down that familiar pit of terror.

"Focus, look at what's in front of you," she said to me. I made the effort to see through the fear. The whole world was blurring and disappearing the same way that it had when I lost myself on the acid trip. I anticipated the chaos with ever-increasing dread. She kept saying, "you already know, you already know, ya sabes, ya sabes."

I tried to focus on my vision. Blackness and chaos dissolved and the world finally came back, to my relief and amazement. I realized she had not laughed maliciously at me. She had laughed to show me how foolish I was. She laughed to show me there was nothing to be scared of. The Bruja came to me to teach me how to cope with my crazy brain.

"Take a deep breath. Focus. Open your eyes. You already know."

It has taken me years to unravel this strange astral event. This was a flying lesson unlike any taught at Hogwarts. She was teaching me how to navigate my own psyche.

Falling becomes a metaphor for every kind of loss of control. Falling means madness, falling means loss of my self and my mind.

Sometimes I don't know who I am. I never felt like I belonged in Mexico because my mother was American and we spoke English at home. My parents read American and British literature to me and we spoke of Western culture. I might have lived in Mexico but I never knew Mexico. I never knew that part of myself. In my heart I was American. I identified with American rock stars and writers. American culture was woven into my perceptual framework.

But when we moved to the suburbs of Chicago I felt completely alienated to a degree I never had before. I had not realized how much of Mexico was in my soul. Even if I did not entirely understand the culture, it was the water that I swam in, it was the air I breathed. I was a part of Puebla the way the bougainvillea bushes were a part of Puebla, because they were born there.

My idea of my self and who I am does not always match up. I let things that people have said to me poison my thoughts. I let the way some people have treated me deform my image of my self. I am not Mexican. I am not American.

I am a child of the universe.

Dreams like this one have shown me that I need to see past the surface of things and that perception is subjective.

I am learning to fly. The voices of self-doubt are only as strong as I let them be. I can laugh at them and laugh at myself, because I might be done with the funhouse mirror but the funhouse mirror is not done with me.

Gracias, Cosmic Bruja, you are always welcome in my dreams.

In the meantime, La Luna illuminates the dark side of my mind while you are off teaching other girls how to fly.

WITH THE BEATING OF THEIR WINGS

MARTEL SARDINA

he monks chant as they carry me to the hillside. They pray for the person I once was and for the person I will become. The sun is bright and its rays are warm. I am naked and cold under this thin cloth shroud. I always thought that the dead could not feel. Some say our bodies are just shells, that it is the spirit that makes us living, breathing beings. When I was a child, I was not sure what to believe. When my father died, I witnessed the moment when he took his last breath. The shell theory made sense to me then. It certainly seemed that his spirit left his body with that final breath. But now that I am on the other side, I believe what the elders believe. The spirit stays with its host until it is released. That's my only explanation for why I am aware that I am still here.

Kalden was the name of my host's body. When the monks finish praying, they set me down in the middle of the stone circle, not far from the temple. I will rest here and watch them as they prepare for the ceremony. Kalden will be buried soon.

The vultures are already circling overhead. Some have landed and start to approach me, but the guardians shake long sticks at them and scare them off.

Three men wearing long, white aprons unwrap my shroud. Their faces are blank of emotion. Only the stoic are meant for this line of work. It's been three days since my death, but they touch me gingerly. Not because my body is stiff and swollen, but because they are being careful not to bump my head and cause my namshe (consciousness) to be released too soon. They cast the shroud aside and pick up their cleavers. In a few short strokes, the blades are made razor sharp by the whetstones.

The men work quickly. They make the necessary cuts. It does not hurt though I do sense a feeling that a part of me has been removed. I hear bones cracking, squishing sounds and plops, as the men retrieve my organs and set them aside.

More vultures have landed. They smell my blood. Their loud squawks are deafening. It is getting harder for the guardians to keep them at bay.

Fortunately, the cutters are done. They give the guardians a hand signal and all of the men fall back and allow the birds to come. There are hundreds of them now. Huge birds that are beautiful and ugly at the same time. Some flap their wings and squawk, hoping to scare the weaker birds away and increase their share. They bite, tug and pull at my flesh. I am in awe of their strength and power.

I hear my mother crying. I wish I could tell her that I am okay. She should not be sad or fear for me. She should know that what has happened and what is about to happen are merely steps in the process. I will make my way through the bardo. She should join the monks in prayer. Seven weeks from now, I will find my new host and have rebirth.

Still, none of this is easy for her. She would not allow me to attend my father's own burial. She said I was too young. Maybe she thought the vultures would frighten me. I had so many questions about his death. She would not answer them. I begged my grandfather to tell me the truth. That's how I know what will happen next.

In less than fifteen minutes, the vultures will have picked my bones clean. Many of the birds will be sated. They will fly away and the flapping of their huge wings will sound like the chugging fits and starts of a locomotive. The weaker ones who fought unsuccessfully to taste my flesh are hungry. They will stay close. The guardians will have to shoo them away again as the cutters prepare what's left of Kalden for his end.

The cutters will gather what's left of my bones and crush them with mallets. They will save my skull for last. They will crack it open and carefully remove my brain. They will crush my skull as they did with the other bones, reducing it to dust. Then, they will take my brain and organs and mix them with flour and the bone dust. The vultures will sit patiently, watching and waiting for the signal to be feeding again. In minutes, what was left of Kalden will be gone.

***

My spirit soars high above the hillside. Somehow, I am one with the vultures. I can see the crowd below dispersing. The ceremony is over. Kalden is gone. Yet I am still here.

The great birds take me on journey to parts of Tibet that I have never seen. The snowcapped mountains are majestic and magnificent. The mountain air is cold but smells sweet. It is hard to convey everything I am seeing and feeling. My flesh was consumed by hundreds of birds. Now I am experiencing the world from hundreds of different viewpoints. It is beyond my comprehension but somehow, I understand. I go where they go. I see what they see. I eat what they eat. There have been other burial ceremonies. I sense other spirits are here with me.

This goes on for some time. Then I start to sense that an ending is coming. But it is not an ending in a strict sense. There is something beyond it. A beginning perhaps. Has it been seven weeks already?

My grandfather never told me what would actually happen when I found my new host. I begged him to tell me, but he said that he couldn't because he didn't honestly know. He hadn't died yet. How could he?

I didn't know what to expect when the time would come. I don't know if it is different for each spirit. This is what happened to me.

One day, when the female vultures laid their eggs, I felt a sense of detachment from the mother birds and a sense of attachment to the eggs. Himalayan vultures lay one egg at a time, but since Kalden had been consumed by many, part of me had been transferred to all of the eggs laid that day.

Some of the eggs eventually hatched and part of me was carried on by a new generation of the great birds. Some of the eggs never hatched and a part of me truly died.

One egg was stolen from its nest by a peasant woman. She took the egg home, cooked and ate it. My spirit melded with hers. When she coupled with her husband, my new host was conceived.

***

My new mother is a simple woman. She calls my host "Pasang" because I was born on a Friday. The elders call me "Keyuri" after the cemetery goddess, because I am always asking questions about life, and life after death. I tell them I had another name once. I don't remember my old host's name anymore. I tell them I was once a boy and that I've soared above the Himalayas on a vulture's wings. The elders believe me.

I tell them that I want to be a cutter.

My mother gets upset when I speak of such things.

"It is a man's job and the elders will not allow it," she says.

But somehow, I know that in this life, that is my destiny.

The elders prayed for guidance. They know that I am more than just a peasant girl. The only way I can be a cutter is if I will hide my true identity.

I shave my head. I bind my breasts to flatten them. I have boyish features and am not petite. It is a relatively easy transformation.

The elders give me a new name.

They call me "Tenzin" now. A fitting name for I will be a protector of Dharma and all of its teachings.

The elders tell my mother that "Pasang" is dead. They don't want any loose ends.

***

The vultures circle overhead.

The monks carry the girl's body to the hillside and place it in the center of the stone circle. I carefully remove her shroud and set it aside as my partners sharpen the cleavers against the rocks in short strokes. My face is blank of emotion. Though I am amazed by how much she looked like Pasang.

The elders are testing me.

If I can make it through this ceremony, avoid reacting to my mother's cries, I will be known as "Tenzin The Cutter" until it is my time to find a new host.

I hear my mother sobbing. I want to tell her that I am okay. But I can't. I know I've had this feeling before. She should not be sad or fear for the life that was. All of us will make it through the bardo when it is our time. We should embrace the opportunity for transformation in the earthly and spiritual realms. These opportunities are our chances for growth.

My partner hands me the cleaver. I straddle my look-alike.

We cut the girl.

The guardians shoo the great birds away with long sticks. They smell her blood. Their squawks are deafening.

I stand and move out of the way when my partner gives the signal to allow the birds to feed.

I watch, awed by the power and strength of their jaws as they rip and tear her flesh away.

My only regret is that I am not the one making the journey skyward.

The ceremony ends.

The great birds fly away. The beating of their wings turns my sadness into peace.

I am careful not to smile.

Though I want to.

DEATHSIDE

ALLYSON BIRD

"And I shall have some peace there, for peace comes dropping slow,
Dropping from the veils of morning to where the cricket sings."
—By kind permission of A. P .Watt Ltd,
on behalf of Grainne Yeats,
from *The Lake of Innisfree, Poems of W. B. Yeats*,
the MacMillan edition 1962.

"When men and women die, other people summon priests, their loved ones, or the doctor. Lorne Delaware wanted me. He said that no one else would be able to see that his wife, Darla, got there safely, to the other side. You see, Captain, I know that it is at the moment of death that the dying are at their most vulnerable for they slip into some dreamlike state. At that moment It could snatch them. Take them, to that no man's land as their soul leaves the body, seconds before they can muster the strength to pass over."

"Are you shitting me?" was the Captain's response. "What off-world notion is that? You're that crazy goon I read about, the one who says that there is something that grabs us when we die."

I shrugged my shoulders. "I can't help it if you don't believe me, Captain. I'm telling the truth as I see it."

"You're damned right I don't believe you."

"But even if you don't believe it, no one should die alone, right?" It was more of a suggestion than a statement.

The Captain thought for a while. "I don't believe a word of what you have said, John Valen, but on the other hand if you want to sacrifice yourself to this virus, then hey—that's your problem. I don't think much of our chances, after what the doctor told me. But once you go into the isolation unit on this ship, you stay there—understand?"

"I understand."

"No one will come out to us from Althea, they are too afraid. Even with stringent quarantine regulations, they won't come. I've asked them." The Captain began to cough. As I left the room he slammed his fist down on the table and his coughing became more persistent.

It was just like the time Darla passed over, but Lorne had more faith in me then. I began to save so many. After that I could have had anything I wanted, status and wealth, but I only wanted one thing, and that was to get away from what I'd seen. To get away from the dark entity that was hungry for souls and haunted the dying. The dying knew real terror and now I knew it too. I was running scared and my fear had caught up with me.

We had been stricken by some alien virus and it was picking us off, one by one. I had told the Captain who I was, for I was afraid for the ship full of families with children. They thought they were on a quick hop to Althea, a planet which was in the Poseidon galaxy, "A Water World Beyond Your Wildest Dreams," the promo declared. In reality, if they all died, they would be facing the greatest journey they had ever taken. Just how was I going to see that they all made it to the Luminary safely?

In these last few weeks, some families complained of a mild sickness but it seemed nothing much to worry about, that is until half the crew became very ill and the travellers started to panic a little. We were only five days away from our destination.

Looking back now I had done everything I could for Darla and Lorne had known that. I had been very close to her, in those last moments as I held her in my arms. I had kept a cool head, not panicked, and never let my guard down once. I had been Darla's bodyguard or rather the guardian of her soul, and delivered her to the Luminary. The Luminary were from another world, for indeed there is one. In fact there are many. I had ensured that Freya Banks had gotten there safely, and I saw her shimmering form dance and smile as they led her away. With John Ryan it was another story. The evil thing (for I had never found a name that could encompass the horror) had descended like a huge black shroud, stifling his soul. When my concentration lapsed and I became weaker, It blighted and withered him away. That is what has haunted me ever since. I wished I could save every soul on Earth, but I knew that was an impossible task.

I was running away again. Lorne was running too and had left Earth a bitter man, mourning the death of his wife. It was to be some sort of new beginning for him and his daughter, Celina, but now they were facing a deadly virus and the other unseen enemy.

That's where I came in. If the worst came to the worst and they died I would try and ensure their safe delivery. I have seen, with my own eyes, a soul snatched from the arms of the Luminary and dragged screaming away. I couldn't stand the thought of that happening to Celina. Then there was me. I was not afraid of dying but what really scared the shit out of me was just who would ensure my safe delivery to the other side?

I had been allowed, once suited up, to sit with the dying. In the last seven days I had won every battle but one. For how long could I carry on? I never left the confines of the isolation unit. Even the Luminary looked worried and that was saying something. If anyone had said to me a year ago that it was possible that there would be this deathside struggle I would have laughed in their face. The entity would surely want me more than anyone else, as I had cheated it so very often.

I did what I could for the dying and then the Captain got really sick. With only an isolation suit between us, we communicated. The Captain was sweating profusely and his hands looked marble-veined. He was only in his mid-thirties but he looked much older at that moment. He struggled to find the words.

"Look—look, John, I have never seen anything like this before. It will pick us off one by one, all of us dead within the next week, unless we do something about it." The Captain coughed and looked like he was going to throw up.

"I don't know what to do," I said.

The Captain could hardly sit up in the bed. "I have no idea how the virus got on board. All I know is that it is highly contagious and if we don't work out what is going on, we either all die on board or we can try again to get help and risk spreading the virus."

I stared out of the window into deep space. "If we all die and someone comes to salvage the ship, won't it spread?"

"I don't know," he said with a sorry shake of his head.

It wasn't the thought of dying that scared me. There are deaths and there are deaths and once in a while there comes along a death that is oh, so special, different in so many certain and profound ways—and that death would be mine. There are no other guardians like me, as far as I know. There would be no one there to free me from Its cold grasp. I didn't know why It couldn't come near me when I was alive, but when I was dead I feared that would be a different matter.

Three days before we reached our destination, more and more of the passengers succumbed to the sickness and panic began to spread. Whole families lay huddled together in corridors and in their quarters, either too sick to move or too terrified to leave for fear of contamination. Three days before—what?

I went to intercede for the Captain. He was unconscious and oblivious to the coming onslaught. I sat down on his bed and waited. I did not have to wait long. Through the visor in my suit I could see the entity moving closer to the Captain. The Captain's death rattle became more pronounced and the black shroud crept closer, threatening to envelop us both. The terror was final: nothing could have made me shake more as It tried to become more manifest. I could see the white-balled eyes fix on us both. The terrible eyes were the only thing that remained constant in Its shifting shape and shroud. I could smell the foulness of it, even inside the suit, as I cradled the dying man in my arms and hoped against hope that the Luminary would come in time. The Captain took one last rattling breath and I could see his body shimmer. There were only seconds to go before his soul would leave his body and the thing would take him away.

I felt myself slipping into unconsciousness as the fear filled my mind. I felt the entity try to take me as well as the Captain. I must fight it. I must. I felt myself giving up, succumbing to the will of something that should not live, that should be dead itself. Then I felt the terror cease and I saw them. The Luminary surrounded us, caressed and reassured us. I saw them take the Captain and I saw the entity retreat before their incredible presence.

After the Captain died and the disease became rampant I saw no reason to stay in the isolation unit. The virus was spreading faster and faster. After all, there was no one to bring the dying to me, so I went to them. I could not get to everyone in their last moments. Whilst attending one family, all dying at the same time, I deserted another but in my desperation at least I never turned to God. I didn't know who the Luminary were but I felt that no man-made religion could readily explain them away. They did not seem to need divine intervention to help them. They seemed like good Samaritans to me, who themselves took a risk to intercede. I believe they are the loved ones of the dead who are drawn back from who knows where? Possibly, they are souls who have had an actual physical connection with the deceased whilst they were alive. I may be wrong. I was an orphan and had spent my formative years in a home where I was careful never to get close to anyone—usually because they went away. No one would be waiting for me.

I deposited the dead in an airlock and ejected them into space. I hoped that the virus would die with them. Their marbled faces a parody of the beautiful Greek statues that were still to be found in the museums on Earth. I felt terrible when Lorne died. His body was dumped into space and floated slowly away with a look of terror fixed firmly on his face. The Luminary hadn't gotten to him in time and I hadn't been there for him either. It had interceded.

One day before we reached our destination, I attended the death of the only other person left alive on the ship. Lorne had died two days earlier and his little girl lay in my arms with her marble-veined hands trying to find some way through my isolation suit to get to me. It was at that point I gave up. Who was I kidding? No one would board the ship as long as there was anyone else alive. Even the salvage crews had left us alone. I took off my gloves and held her little hand in mine. I may have been tired but there was no way It was going to get at her. There was no sign of the entity. It was not long before the Luminary came to take her away. Amongst them was Darla, for it was her little daughter, Celina, who had just died.

Soon it would be my turn. I was the last man standing. I felt what it was like to be truly alone. Althea was only a day away but I might as well have been on the other side of the universe. I started to cough and tasted blood in my mouth. I looked down at my hands and saw that they had taken on a blue-white hue and felt myself weakening. I could make out the dark shape of the entity starting to form. There would be no Luminary for me, to light my way to another world. I had been alone in life and I would be alone in death, except for It that waited, biding its time for my life to slip away. At least Celina would be safe.

My breathing became more labored and my dying breath was upon me. It left in three long drawn-out gasps and gently I set myself free of my earthly body, and faced the entity. I was too weak after this rebirth to move. I felt as thin as air but unable to do anything as It came closer. The impenetrable blackness crept forward towards me. It hesitated as a great light began to fill the room. I felt some of my energy return and I managed to drift round towards the light.

It was such a beautiful sight, for there before me, was every soul I had ever saved, old and young alike. Amongst the hundreds I could see those of Darla and little Celina. It was Celina who then held out her tiny hands to me.

THLUSH-A-LUM

REBECCA GOMEZ FARRELL

Markella's earliest memories are of the sounds outside her window. At hours when no men moved, rustling branches and shuffling grass woke her. A beating pulse like slower, fleshier helicopter blades banished sleep: thlush-a-lum thlush-a-lum. In summers, the heat in her attic bedroom hot enough to incubate, Markella pushed the window open and dozed to the endless static drone of cicadas. In winters, choking radiator warmth wrapped tight around her, she cracked the window and the low, deep hoots of an owl drifted in with the freezing breeze.

The sounds crept in no matter the season. She did not know then that the noise of a UFO landing might be only the wind whipping through the woods. Or that the piercing cries of something caught in a monster's jaws were likely car wheels screeching too fast past the roundabout. The unknowns terrified little Markella, curled up so tight on her bed that she'd spring like a can of snakes if touched. But no one touched her. Mother and Father had no patience for tucking her in or answering her questions about how winds and teakettles could both whistle. Even the dog, a playful chocolate lab that dug joyfully at every ant hill it encountered, offered no more than a whimper when Markella ventured near.

As she grew older, Markella learned to tell the difference between sounds. Wasps buzzed like a kazoo while carpenter bees plucked a bass. Snow fell quieter than rain, and a pan sizzled differently if there was oil in it rather than water. She took comfort in naming the noises that woke her, in having something to think of until silence and sleep came again. Loud crack like a gun gone off? An ash tree breaking in two. Knocking on the side of the house? A woodpecker looking for an early morning snack. The noises had a purpose, an action they belonged to unlike Markella, never quite belonging, never quite her parents' daughter.

***

Thlush-a-lum.

Thlush-a-lum.

She never has figured out what makes the noise of the helicopter blades. It wakes her tonight, resonating like leather and bone, not metal. Markella's eyes snap open as she takes in the color of darkness seeping into her room, reddish-purple like the Chianti Mother gave her at dinner with whispers of "growing up" and "transformation," a rare smile spreading beneath her heavy-lidded eyes.

THLUSH-a-lum.

THLUSH-a-lum.

Markella bolts up in bed—it is so loud. She doesn't think it's ever been this loud before. A breath of relief escapes when the noise stops. But a scratching, then slow scraping, replaces it. The window—there's something at the window.

She looks.

Mottled grey hands grasp the wooden, peeling window sill. Yellowed, cracking fingernails click against the glass as the frame inches higher. Wood grates against wood. Immense wings fill the rectangle of the window—two, no, four of them grouped on the creature's shoulders and hips. Something black as motor oil drips from them.

Markella doesn't want to keep looking, but it is too late. She knows that, watching a sinewy leg covered in the same slick substance as the wings push through the opening between frame and sill. The wings begin rotating, each in opposite directions, like gearworks of a clock.

THLUSH-a-lum.

THLUSH-a-lum.

The creature rises high enough to slip the rest of its form inside.

Markella knows in this moment that some noises cannot be explained away, that squealing tires never do sound like screams when she hears them in the light of day. The creature opens its mouth, revealing two rows of teeth as sharp and pointed as the icicles that hang over her window's awning in winter. Those teeth glisten as the dripping wings block out the night sky. The creature emits a high-pitched shriek that makes the dog bark again and again.

She feels shearing pain at the same time as hearing a sickening slurtch. The dimples on her shoulders and lower back—Mother had called them birthmarks—split open and slimy, leathery, skin-covered bones thrust out. Her arms shrink in on themselves, the fat between skin and bone oozing out in minuscule black droplets. Fingernails lengthen and harden as she twists her hands around and around, mesmerized.

Cool air shifts across her back from the wings beginning to rotate and flutter, and Markella stands. The creature's head cocks, eyelids clicking over its pearlescent, oval eyes. Its image divides and multiplies into a million little screens, Markella's vision compounded. Feet curve and toes bind together into a ballet shoe of flesh. When she lifts off the ground, the breeze from the window tickles her soles.

The creature flies outside, moonlight a beacon off its wings. Markella does not hesitate; the desire to propel herself upward, higher and higher, is much stronger than the lingering pain of burst skin. As she jumps out the window and into the open air, she wonders how hurtling through a cloud will sound. The soft noise of untried wings is added to the night sky around her: thlush-a-lum thlush-a-lum.

***

Hidden in the curve of the front alcove, the mother watches her latest charge disappear until it is no more than the speck she wishes it were. She prays it is the last, prays she will not wake to a new larva shaped like the human baby they had bartered for so long ago. Back inside, she pulls the cork from another bottle with a soft pop.

"Is it done?" Her husband sits up on the couch in front of a blank blue television screen. "The dog has stopped barking."

She nods, swishing the wine and watching the film it secretes on the bowl.

"Will they let us go, you think? That's the third one, and they said—"

Her laugh is bitter. "They said that after the first one, too. You can't count on an insect's promises."

The lab comes running, teeth gripping a slobbery rubber ball. It squeaks as he drops it at her feet, whining. She tosses it, launches it far into the darkened hall. The dog scampers away, cartilage claws scuffing the hardwood floor. The mother sighs, her hand already lowered to take it again. It'll come back. It always does.

THE FALLEN

PAMELA JEFFS

The breeze raises dust from the dirt road. There's no haste in the motion, only a slow red bloom of particles that curls up and hangs for an instant before falling back and settling into place. It's the only movement in a sparse desert landscape made up of red dirt and the scattered skeletons of long-dead trees.

Other than the sound of the wind, and the ocean booming away against the far coast, the world is silent. No humans, no animals, no life. Nothing sentient except me.

It's midday and the sun is blistering overhead. My mouth is dry. I reach for my oil bottle, the liquid inside sloshing as I tip it up to drink. Only two mouthfuls before it empties. Time to head back home for more. I return the bottle and press the button on my wrist.

Engage.

A click and a whir, and my mechanical wings extend. Their metal length gleams in the midday heat. I kick off from the dead earth and am airborne.

The wind whines and shrieks past my ears. I tip my left aileron and wheel toward the coast. The water sparkles in the distance.

Ingrained habit has me searching the ground as I go. I've been doing this for a hundred long years. Searching. I don't really expect to find anyone anymore, but my programming maintains my drive.

Seek out humanity. Search and salvage.

And so I, Ena Unit, prototype robotic search-and-rescue android, search. It was the purpose given to me by the scientists at the Institute of Life for Humanity. I was the only android they had the parts to perfect; I was their only hope. Find and rescue any humans who survived the final world war. That was my duty.

But I was doomed to failure. Those scientists, they sent me out too late. The chemical wars had already torn the world apart by the time I arrived. All that was left were the toxins—toxins that eventually killed every living thing.

The last living human had been my mother, for want of a name, she who designed and activated me. She was Athena Panos, an industrial designer. Her last words still ring in my ears.

"You are alpha and omega, Ena," she said, "the beginning and the end. Take what's left of the world and make it yours."

I often think of when she died; the feeling of her aged fingers slipping free of my wrist; the faraway look that manifested in her eyes. I buried her in the fashion of her people: deep in the ground, cradled by warm earth. It was what she would have wanted, I think.

After that, I left the facility. I couldn't bear to stay. The silence within its concrete walls was overwhelming.

My thoughts are drowned out as my eye catches a glint of light below me: a flash of white against the red desert. Mechanical debris. I tilt my wings and descend.

Working parts are now the only things I search for. And here I've found a fallen drone. Half buried in the sand, the circular machine is battered and yet it holds promise. Its eight rotor blades are rusted to nondescript lumps of ore, but the outline of letters marked on the weathered plastic casing can still be seen: DAx25.

I search my data banks. The information is easy to find. It's a cloud-seeding drone, and was manufactured in the year 2200 for the purpose of helping to increase rainfall over desert areas.

I run my fingers across her curved lines. "Hello, pretty lady," I whisper.

I lever my fingers in beneath the edge of the drone's carcass and pull it free. A curtain of dirt and rocks cascades over my boots. The grit rises in a blinding cloud, interrupting my vision sensors for a moment. They soon clear. The drone is free of her grave.

She is a meter in diameter. Not large and not heavy, which is a good thing. I turn her over. The twisted mess of rusted wiring and plastic looks to be impossible, but I can see past all that. There is only one part I'm interested in and there's a good chance it's still intact.

I grip the drone with both hands and resume my flight. I no longer scan the ground as I fly, but head straight for the coast.

***

It's loud inside my sea cave. The crash of waves as they pound the shore below the cliffs reverberates like thunder off the salt-slick stone. I know salt is not good for working machinery, but I can't help but be drawn to this place. I like the sound of it. The roar and boom. It drowns out the silence of the world, and in hearing it, I don't feel so lonely.

I gently lay out the drone on my workbench. I tease at the seam in the casing. The weatherworn plastic cracks apart like an eggshell to reveal the inner workings. A nested tumble of seized wiring and plastic components stares back at me. My metal fingers have no problem digging through them to the core of the machine. Rust and dirt trickles past my touch and onto my bench.

Then I find it. The component: small, smooth, still intact. My heart gears begin to whir faster. I curl my fingers around the spherical part and pull it free: the drone's brain-core module.

There's something strange about the metal casing. The stainless steel is pitted with corrosion. The marks are unlike anything I've ever seen. They are green, and track unevenly along the surface of the module like human veins. And my thermal sensors detect warmth in the metal. Not warmth that has come by the sun, but the warmth I remember as belonging to the living, to the humans.

I trace my finger along the marks. The metal is impregnated with corrosion. Perhaps years of contact with the chemicals in the earth have changed it somehow.

I turn and rummage through the oilcans that line the shelf behind my bench. The first two are empty, but the third rewards me with the satisfying glugging sound of clean oil swilling in the bottom. I pull out a dented bathing tray and pour in the oil. I hold back from emptying the can and take only a mouthful. I lift the can and swallow. I relish the thick liquid as it trickles down my throat, coating and cleaning away from my gears the dust collected from the day.

I place the empty oilcan on the bench and lift the drone's module. It slips silently out of my fingers and into the bowl. I imagine I can hear a sigh from the component as the soothing bath soaks and loosens frozen data chips. I smile. It's been a long time since I've had access to enough oil to have an immersive bath. But my memory of it is treasured.

I turn toward the pallet that's laid out next to the bench. The long board is supported by the rugged bulk of two water-worn boulders.

On it, a human-shaped figure lies covered with a salt-rimed canvas cover.

The cover falls away stiffly. The glint of well-oiled metal follows. Long, supple legs, and arms ending in fine fingers lie lax against the weathered pallet board. Two long silver wings are neatly folded at each side of the mechanical body. A face made of smooth, copper-colored metal faces the ceiling. The molded eyes are closed.

I reach over and unhinge the face. It falls to the left and hangs like a type of grotesque metal mask. Inside, the wiring and an empty brain-core module cradle are exposed. After a century in my care, the parts still look new.

I turn back to the oil bath and pull the drone's component clear. Oil, now tarnished green, drips through my fingers and onto the stone floor. I use a rag to wipe away the excess.

I hesitate as I hold the module over the open cradle. This moment feels frozen. I've waited so long for the chance to activate the sister android I salvaged from the facility: Thea Unit. With her by my side, I will no longer be alone on this dead planet. I have dreamt of our conversations, of the endless days we will spend gliding together through empty, sunlit skies.

I lean over. The module clicks into place.

I close the faceplate.

I wait.

The first sign of activation is the flexing of her metal fingers. Then a mechanical sigh whispers out over polished metal lips.

My heart gears quicken.

Her eyes open.

Something is wrong.

Thea's eyes aren't the typical plastic lenses of an android. They are human. Green. Moist. Alive.

I stumble backwards, trying to process what I'm seeing. Thea sits upright, the movement swift, clean. My gears skip a frantic beat. This is not right. Then her pale eyes swivel. Her uncanny gaze locks onto mine. Her mouth opens as if to speak, but then she screams, the sound like that of gears shearing apart.

I watch as her metal skin begins to tarnish. Her silver and copper casings turn dull, the colors shifting to become ash-grey and brown. Green veins appear, etching themselves into her stained metal. She screams again, but this time it sounds almost human. Then her metal skin peels apart.

I watch in horror as the pistons and shock absorbers that constitute her skeleton are revealed. The exposure of her working parts is obscene. But worse still are the slowly growing sheets of flesh, seething and crawling to cover her.

Thea's body quivers, a response I recognise as pain, something no mechanical should feel. Then she falls still. The flesh stops growing. Her half-flesh, half-metal chest rises and falls as she gulps air into lungs she should not own.

Half metal, half flesh, her body is unfinished.

"Thea Unit?" My voice is rusty. I haven't used it in over a century.

The sound draws her gaze to mine.

I recoil from her human eyes; the watching of irises that contract and widen in the uncertain light of the cave. Slowly, gingerly, Thea swings her legs off the pallet. Real fingernails scrape against the timber as her fingers flex.

"Who are you?" she asks.

"Ena Unit," I reply. "Salvage, Search and Rescue."

"Search and Rescue?" Thea laughs, a too-human sound.

My gears suddenly feel dry. I wish I could have another mouthful of oil.

Thea smiles; her once-copper teeth are visible behind her flesh-pink lips. Her teeth look to be stained brown. "So, did you search and rescue me? Salvage me?"

"Yes. Parts of you were salvaged from elsewhere in order to make you functional."

Suddenly her voice is hard, unkind. "You should have left me where I was." She points at her chest. "This body is an abomination." Her face is set like stone; she looks as if she wants to attack me.

I take a step back. My heel catches the edge of an empty oil-can. It clatters away.

Thea pushes herself off the pallet. The skin-covered stumps of her wings hang uselessly by her side; two once-elegant sails now heavy with flesh.

I retreat further, watching as her metal parts—neck, patches of torso and one leg—catch and absorb the light. The rest of her body, the parts covered in flesh, is blushed pink.

"You idiot," she says. "You don't even know what you've done, do you?"

I feel the damp cave wall at my back. I can retreat no further. "What I have done?"

Thea scoffs; her green eyes flare. "I was a seeding drone," she says, as if that admission explains everything.

"Yes. A DAx25 model," I say. "A cloud-seeding drone."

"No." The word hangs like acid in the air. "I was modified. I was a human-seeding drone sent out by the Institute of Life for Humanity. The core-brain module you put in this body was full of human genomes."

The green corrosion on the component suddenly makes

sense. The module was leaking. That's why Thea's body remains incomplete: one hundred years of exposure had stolen part of the dose. There hadn't been enough left to effect a full change to the host body.

I try to explain, "You—"

But she won't let me talk. "No, it's you," she says. "You've wasted humanity's last shot at existence on this stupid metal body."

I have no opportunity to explain. I watch Thea wheel away, her anger crackling like electricity. She stalks to the cave entrance, climbs out over the rocks and leaves. My programming screams at me to go after her, to save her, but there's another part of me that knows this world is no place for the living, and that it's already too late for Thea.

But I have to try.

I burst into action, my metal boots clanging and scraping against the rocks in my frantic effort to catch her. I clear the entrance to the cave, but misjudge my step. The rocks outside are slippery. My foot skids sideways and I tumble over a small ledge of ocean-battered rock. The sky and sea pinwheel in my field of view: blue, green, blue.

I'm lying wedged between two boulders with the sound of pounding surf roaring around me. Salt and sea foam sprays across my face. The buttery texture of oil coats my lips.

Diagnostics: I am damaged. Shattered leg. Crushed chest. Critical leak somewhere deep inside.

I need to get to the cave, to my surplus parts, but I can't get this body back alone.

I look around. And then I see her.

Thea is only meters away. She is sitting on a rock, her metal hand clutched to her chest. She is doubled over. I see her glance up. Her gaze catches mine. I see her cough. I can't hear the sound over the surf, but I see the sudden, bright spray of scarlet blood coat her lips and chin. Then, with herculean effort, she gets to her feet.

Her steps are unsteady as she navigates her way across to me. She says nothing as she grabs my wrist and begins to drag me out of the rocks. I try to help, using my good leg to kick myself free. Slowly she pulls me out, a sheen of oil slicking the water-wet rocks behind me in shades of blue, pink and green. My leg dangles, and sparks fly as she drags me further across the unforgiving terrain. The scrape of my metal skin over the stones is louder than the waves.

Thea gets me to the cave. Now inside, I can hear the heavy rasp of her breath as it struggles in and out of her half-formed lungs. I can feel her uneven pulse in the palm that grips my wrist so tightly. The human part of her is dying, but the mechanical in her is keeping her going, for the moment.

She drags me up onto the pallet. It's a struggle, but her android muscles have more strength than a human's. Once I'm laid out, she pauses for a moment, her head resting against my good leg. "Damn it, but you're heavy."

"I'm made of metal."

She laughs, a tired sound. I watch as she reaches down. Her human hand closes over her own metal leg. A series of clicks and suddenly she pulls it free of her body. She braces herself against the pallet and places the leg on my chest.

"I can't," she says.

So I sit upright, hold the spare leg and detach my damaged one. I click the new one into place just as Thea slides to the floor. While bad, the damage to my chest will have to wait. I recognise that Thea's need is now more urgent. I slip off the pallet and gently kneel by her side.

Her eyes flutter open. "I'm sorry, Ena, I know this isn't your fault." She coughs. More blood. "These humans...so many emotions...so much pain."

I want to understand, but my programming has limits. I have no reference for identifying how it feels to be human. So I do the only thing I can for her; the thing I once did for another. I sit next to her and hold her hand as she lies dying.

Long moments pass. The sound of waves swelling rumbles against the rocks outside, the wind whines.

Then Thea breathes a final, labored breath. Her eyes close.

And just like that, I am alone again.

Omega.

The last.

And even with the noise of the sea around me, the silence of the world is suddenly deafening.

AND WHEN SHE WAS BAD

NADIA BULKIN

Thebe final girl alive sits down on the dark soil and moans. It's her virginal moan, the one that makes her special, but now, three days later, there is no hint of an orgasmic lilt in her voice. It's fatigue that the earthworms in the dirt hear. There is no one else to hear. The others are dead and the strange white-haired couple whose land this has been since the Civil War are dead, and so are all their animals, even the sad-eyed German shepherd. Even the chickens' eggs have their tops bitten off and their insides sucked dry, so not even the unborn hear how her voice has changed. The monster, does he hear? She looks at him, broken-legged and broken-winged in front of the barn where he killed her slutty best friend. Poor dead Ann, always a little wild. She promised they were on the road to Aspen. She promised no wrong turns.

***

Thirty minutes later, the final girl wipes her own blood on her face and stands and goes to the monster. He knows no words and begs for nothing as she comes close—his torsal wound has clotted all dark and ugly, and his broken leg has swollen, and if he is a product of nature then he must be in pain. She did not think he was, earlier. She thought he really had spawned from Hell, and she had been hating herself as she hid under the bed and he ate the old woman on top for not being able to remember a single Scripture after spending twelve years in the basement of a church embedding them in her heart. The mattress had bowed down on her back like the pressure of God, or if it was her granola self talking, karma. She thought about her sins and Sodom and Gomorrah and celestial wrath raining down on the plain, washing it of all the devils, and like a good little angel she bit her lower lip bloody and felt the pain and sucked it back in. And then she ran over the monster with a hay baler and broke half his body and realized he was mortal after all. Angel's got herself a sickle now. Everybody's bleeding, everybody's dead. Everybody's made of iron and water and bone.

***

The final girl and the monster go to the nearest town. She's going to bring him to justice, that's what she told him. Going to make sure he never hurts anyone again. She ran him over a second time to be certain and then chained him to the baler and drove it up to the little country road, dragging him behind her. His face is in the gravel. They pass the car that Ann's boyfriend tried to escape to—its tires are still slashed out and Josh is still half in the windshield, with his feet chewed off.

The final girl did not even like Josh the drunken frat boy, but she still screams back at the monster, "Look at that! Look at what you did, you sick freak! Look at it!" And she regrets not doing the same thing for Ann, down in the barn. But the monster's face is in the gravel and the monster sees nothing. He learns nothing. He is after all the monster. The final girl feels her ribs compress and little by little she starts to cry. They're anguished tears, the kind of tears she expected when she was trapped in a storage room with the monster breaking in, not the kind of tears appropriate for this moment in her narrative. Now she is free, and the terror is crippled at her feet, and the sky is laid bare and swallows, thin birds, are crossing overhead like little flourishes of hope. Yet she cries and cries and the monster does not respond, and she looks back over and over at the car and then down the hill at the grungy farm, left to languish in the putrid smell of death. She wishes she was dragging back the right bodies and cries some more because this brutality is what she has. This is her prize for being good, this is what was behind door number three, this is her gold star sticker. She keeps her foot on the pedal as her chest keeps heaving and the baler groans on like nothing is happening.

***

The baler stops. It put-puts to a halt as the dark comes in over the trees, and at first the final girl just sits on the uncomfortable little stool, scared to look behind her although she's been listening to the monster drag over the asphalt for the past two hours. Now the two of them have lost all civilization, because the farm is gone and the nearest town, that fabled myth, has not come into view. But then she picks up the sickle she's kept under her foot and gathers the strength to turn and look at the monster. She imagines him standing, his jaws fallen open and dripping saliva, ready to consume her headfirst. But he is not—he is still lying on the road, twitching occasionally.

She hears in the black woods by the road a miniature howl and begins to think of other monsters: coyotes, wolves. She wonders what he is, this savage thing. She hates that he eats parts of his victims, but this trait of his also reminds her of the Big Bad Wolf and oddly enough, this consoles her. Maybe he is just an animal, like the Beast of Bray Road and the Ozark Howler. Maybe he is just wired to prey on other creatures. Maybe it's not his fault. This idea makes it easier for her to envision killing him too. It's what's always been done to rabid animals, to dogs with mange, to escaped leopards, to pit bulls that bite little babies.

Dumb beasts, she thinks, remembering her uncle putting down a horse with a broken leg. Dumb beasts can't help it and we can't help them. She tries to breathe calmly and accept her role as executioner of this thing she has captured. But her uncle let that horse go gently into the night, with a tranquilizer and a syringe, and all she has is a sickle. That's a weapon with no pity. She decides the townspeople, when she finally reaches them, will carry out the grisly job themselves. What would her parents say if she came home with blood on her hands? Still, she keeps pity in her heart and nurses it like a kitten. She's always felt pity for the strangest things. For dying insects. For hitchhikers ambling down the road looking lost. Earlier on this trip—before the wrong turn—she chastised Josh for mocking those lost souls, and Ann of course mocked her in turn. "Such delicate sensibilities," her mother used to say, brushing her hair.

Feeling relieved, the final girl gets off the stool and quickly unhooks the chain from the baler, then starts to drag. He's lighter than she thought he'd be.

***

The final girl hates that the monster does not talk. All afternoon she thinks, talk, monster, talk. It is possible that he is dead and has been all this time, and that those little tics and flutters of his ragged wings are tricks of moonlight or her own wishful thinking. She's not willing to close the gap between them to check. Instead she just hates him from afar. She would not care if he talked about eating people or how he was going to kill her or how it felt when he killed Ann. She hates her own company much more. Why the hell else would she say yes to Aspen with Ann and Josh if they weren't a reprieve from the deafening white solitude of her dorm room, perched ten stories above the ground like the bell tower of Notre Dame? But the monster has never spoken. He is, after all, the monster.

She says, "I could tell you my life story." He says nothing. "I was born in Grand Forks. I had good parents. I go to college now. I'm an English major." She stops because her own life makes her hair stand on end. There is nowhere to go with that story. "I could tell you why I survived." He says nothing. He drags, that's what he says, his scrapes against the ground are his reply. She imagines it's his way of saying yes. "I survived because I am a good girl. I am not a slut. I am not a pig. I am not…" She thinks of the old couple whose house the car broke down in front of, who narrowed their beady little eyes at them, this pack of teenagers in threadbare clothes, but let them in anyway. "I am not old and stupid. And I can run. I always got good grades. And my father taught me how to…" She remembers her father clapping and laughing after she finished singing the national anthem in the living room, how he said, "Good girl! Good girl!" Her voice trickles off as she watches the moon and the moon watches her. "And it doesn't matter," she finishes.

The monster doesn't reply. She keeps dragging. The stress on her joints burns out all those things she just said, the things that don't matter. The memories of blood and screaming and slamming doors and slipping keys and shotgun cocks fade with every step. The great big amorphous past has risen up behind them on the country road and is swallowing those memories whole. When she thinks of them now all she feels is numb release. It is leaving a long hollowness where her sternum should be. A void. She realizes the chorus that she thought was the moon clucking actually belongs to cicadae in the long grass.

"You see? Even animals can talk," she says, looking back at him. Her voice is quivering. Inside she's begging him to say something. Just a grunt would do. When Ann and Josh left her in the farmhouse to go fuck in the barn she was actually happy to hear the monster land on the roof with a screech that sent the animals into hysterics—else she'd have to listen to her own little voice all night. He drags along.

***

It is night and the dog comes soundlessly from behind. The final girl thinks she hears a growl but as she's turning she gets jerked off her feet and falls. She's lucky the sickle in her hand doesn't tear through her thigh. Her wrist is still being tugged while her head is throbbing and instinctively she pulls back on the chain—it takes her a minute to turn over onto her stomach and see that some kind of stray hunting mutt has the monster by the neck and is trying to drag him off the road.

"Hey!"

The dog glances up at her with urine-colored eyes but it only lasts a second. It's the raggedy monster it wants.

No, she thinks. No, he's mine. She's not sure why she thinks this, but she tells herself it's because she wants to own the coming vengeance, she wants to personally ensure the nearest town burns him alive in the name of Ann and Josh and the McFaydens, she wants to feel the heat of the pyre. She tells herself it's because the monster hasn't killed this stupid dog's friends.

With her heart in her throat, she yanks the chain back again and with the other hand lunges for the dog with the sickle. The final girl bites her lip because already the dog is drawing blood—dark and viscous, it leaks from under the monster's rubbery chin—and she's afraid she's too late.

Then the monster lifts up one clawed, previously dormant hand and grabs the dog's neck. The final girl skids to a rough stop and watches as the dog, suddenly whimpering, gets its neck twisted until its head is barely hanging off its body. The monster starts eating, loud and visceral like he's not ashamed. After ten minutes, the monster throws the mangled body at the stricken young woman. It hits her sneakers but she's seen so much carnage recently that it doesn't even make her jump. She just kicks the offering aside and marches up, shaking, to the monster she thought was crippled. By the time she's leaning over him and her hair has fallen down into grabbing range he's laid down on his back again and closed his eyes. Seeing this elicits a staggered shriek.

"What, are you surrendering now?" She gives the chain a hard yank and the monster's head flops in response. He doesn't wake. His arms and knees have tucked into his body like a baby in a womb. She lifts the sickle. "I'm going to kill you, you idiot!"

The monster opens his eyes. One dig of the sickle will end his life and she can't believe he doesn't know this, being a monster. Still he throws up no defense. His bloody lips don't even hiss.

"Why won't you kill me?" This, she says softer. He did try to, earlier—but he never seemed to put as much effort into killing her as he put into killing Ann and Josh and the McFaydens. He always seemed to miss. He always seemed to give her time to run. And this makes her drop her sickle. Her shoulders slump and her knees go wobbly. "Why me, huh? Why do I get to be the last girl? You don't care about how good I am, you don't care about…" She shakes her head, because all he could have seen in her was a trembling piece of teenaged meat. "You're a fucking monster."

The monster is back to feigning death and subservience and will not communicate with her. She starts walking away, pulling the chain taut. "What, are you lonely?" she asks. She says it sarcastically, but as soon as the words are out there she knows they're true. The monster doesn't reply as she begins once again to drag it down the empty road. The shock of suddenly having something in common with a creature so awful silences the girl he let live, and she wipes her eyes on her muddy sleeve. There's been no cars on this road all day. But then again it was a wrong turn.

***

Sometime between nightfall and sunrise she stops walking and sits down, then lies down. There's no more dragging sounds and the silence bites her now. The monster turns over and folds his good wing over his head. The chain between them is not stretched taut and still he shows no interest in eating her. The final girl is thinking that maybe he should have eaten her; but she thinks this cautiously, afraid that he will somehow hear her thoughts and come on over, jaws gaping, ready to obey.

"You ate all my friends. I have no one now," she whispers at the lump she holds hostage. But she knows she was lonely long before the monster first landed on the roof of the farmhouse like an angel of pestilence. She was lonely long before she went to college and became Ann's roommate (the only reason Ann dragged her along on this trip—it was out of pity). Could people be born lonely? She remembers being lonely even back in kindergarten when all children are supposed to be delightful little cherubs, that is why she wonders. Well, time is nothing. How the void inside began doesn't matter. All that matters is that it's there.

The monster just let her scream about it. The monster let her run. He let her pound her heels into the ground and her heart into her ribs, so angry and vicious and alive, this sweating ugly little girl in the mud with dirt under the fingernails and grease in her hair was now finally filled with real bursting pain, the stuff that burned so much cleaner than internal sorrow. The monster let her bleed. The monster let her swing baseball bats and rip clothes and howl like the Beast of Bray Road herself. He let her break bones and he let her like it. He let her swear. She has said fuck more times in the past three days than she has in all her twenty years of life and each time it's felt like a breaking wave. Doing all that sick ugly nasty stuff has been like vomiting the sad lonely years with their pastel colors and blue ribbons and dutiful pats on the head for the good little girl.

The final girl digs her filthy nails into her skin and wonders what she was really trying to run over with that hay baler when she jammed her foot against the pedal and screamed, "Die, you piece of shit! Die!"

"Why did you come here?" she asks the monster that is barely a monster anymore. "Did I invite you somehow? Did I dream you into being?"

Only the void inside responds.

She is afraid that the monster is her golem, and that is why he never talks. But if that is true, he has done well. That she can't argue. The skeleton that is left of her bottled life feels unbelievably clean after the three-day orgy of violence, like boiled bones. That night she sleeps not curled up like a scared snail but open wide. Insects crawl in her hair and nest, as if she is their queen mother.

***

All night she dreams of fists. Every time they are her own. She recognizes her bony knuckles, cut up from punching through the glass of a door that wouldn't open back at the McFaydens' farmhouse. In her dream she is punching through wooden doors too. She is coming down out of a crystalline sky and punching red shingles. She punches the leathery skin of a cow. She punches rib cages and faces and stomachs of people she thinks she might know. She watches them crash. She punches the mattress. She punches the monster; his jaw crunches like it's made of styrofoam. She punches herself. And there's a voice in her dream that sounds like her own saying "Arise, arise!"

There's Ann, dying in front of her. There's the bed that she tears the stuffing from. Late in the dream, when the colors are bleeding and the American Gothic portraits are shuddering down the wall, she is in a bathroom. She looks down and sees that her fingernails have gone black and that she is barefoot. She looks in the mirror and it cracks.

***

In the morning the monster is awake. He is watching her with his blank reptilian eyes. She looks back at him as he sits cross-legged on the center stripe of the road. She somewhat hopes he'll speak but is barely disappointed when he doesn't—as usual, she speaks instead. "I'm going to let you go," she says. "How do you feel about that?" The monster has no reaction, of course. "I'm going to let you go, but only if you give me what I want." He has no objection and she moves closer.

She takes off his tattered devil's wings. She puts them on.

Without them he looks like a shriveled fetus, a burned giraffe, something that was not meant to be and that life was finally, mercifully letting go. He curls up as he watches her adjust his wings. A couple rolls of the shoulder and they feel right. She can feel the wind seeping in through the tears, and one of them has been bent up something awful by the hay baler, but she still gives them a go. She flaps and imagines the monster swooping down and catching the old man and eating him, mid-flight, like an eagle with a hare—she wonders if that will be as hard as it looks. She flaps harder and the wind catches her. With difficulty, the final girl rises a few feet off the ground and awkwardly sways in the breeze.

The woeful little thing below her, purposeless now, emits a strange, guttural squawk and lifts up his webbed fingers. His neck is still tied to the chain and he's starting to get pulled upward the higher she goes. He doesn't want to follow her forever. She unravels the chain from around her hand. She drops it and watches the creature meekly crawl away, wondering what to do with himself now that she has no need for him, until a higher wind rises and takes her over the trees. In the distance she sees a farmhouse, and swoops. She is used to flying solo.

COPYRIGHT ACKNOWLEDGMENTS

ABOUT THE EDITOR

Amber Fallon lives in Massachusetts with her husband and two dogs. A techie by day and horror writer by night, Mrs. Fallon has spent time as a bank manager, motivational speaker, produce wrangler, and butcher. Her obsessions with sushi, glittery nail polish, and sharp objects have made her a recognized figure.

Amber's publications include *The Warblers, The Terminal, Sharkasaurus, Daughters of Inanna, So Long and Thanks for All the Brains, Horror on the Installment Plan, Zombies For a Cure, Quick Bites of Flesh, Operation Ice Bat,* and more! *Fright Into Flight* is her first anthology.

For more information, please visit her at www.amberfallon.net.